DEMONS IN THE NIGHT
RESURRECTION

HEATHER GALE

This is a work of fiction. Names, characters, places, and incidents are products of the author's imagination or are used fictitiously and are not to be construed as real. Any resemblance to actual events, locations, organizations, or persons, living or dead, is entirely coincidental.

World Castle Publishing, LLC
Pensacola, Florida
Copyright © Heather Gale 2021
Paperback ISBN: 9781953271761
eBook ISBN: 9781953271778
First Edition World Castle Publishing, LLC, March 1, 2021
http://www.worldcastlepublishing.com
Licensing Notes
Cover: Karen Fuller
Editor: Maxine Bringenberg

CHAPTER 1

A gentle breeze blew by as Michelle stood, completely speechless, in the woods facing Rubeus. Her body was frozen and her eyes wide, on the verge of tears, as she tried to determine if this was real or a dream.

"You were dead," Michelle managed to get out.

Alyssa finally found them and skidded to a halt. She crossed her arms and narrowed her eyes at him.

"I should have been," Rubeus said, hesitant to take a step towards her. "I can only guess you got to me in time and returned the energy I gave you."

"Well, where did you go?" Michelle asked.

Rubeus glanced over at Alyssa. She was now glaring at him and mouthed the word "no" to him. He looked away.

"I…was in a coma," Rubeus finally answered. "I woke about a month ago and have been building my strength back."

Michelle closed the distance and wrapped her arms around him. He embraced her back.

"I *knew* it!" Trevin yelled as he found them. Michelle and Rubeus let each other go as Alyssa and Trevin came up to them. Trevin and Rubeus hugged. "I knew there was no way."

"Yeah, I can't believe you're here," Alyssa replied, but

with a hidden meaning. Rubeus and Alyssa made eye contact once more.

"I'll catch up with you guys later." Rubeus pulled Michelle back to him.

"Please do," Alyssa responded, crossing her arms.

Trevin glanced over at Alyssa. "What's with the attitude towards him?" Trevin asked once Michelle and Rubeus were gone.

"I didn't have an attitude," Alyssa stated simply as she turned to leave. Trevin grabbed her above the elbow, she looked back.

"You knew."

"Don't be ridiculous," Alyssa responded, pulling her arm free as they started to walk out of the woods.

Trevin grabbed her arm again. "No, you weren't surprised at all." Trevin pulled her to a stop. "You had an irritated expression the entire time. You knew he was alive." Alyssa stood silent and pulled out of his grasp again. "Michelle's gonna be pissed at you if she finds out."

"She'll be more upset with Rubeus for lying to her," she snapped.

"Rubeus wouldn't lie to her," Trevin said sternly. "Not about that."

"Well, he just did. He wasn't in a coma," Alyssa said with a very smug tone. "He was alive and well for the past eight months."

"Where was he then?" Trevin questioned. "And why let everyone think he was dead?"

"The dead part wasn't supposed to happen, but it worked out better with it." Alyssa stepped out of the woods and into the clearing by the river. "I can't tell you where he was, so please just drop it."

"So he was on a secret mission." Trevin shrugged. "Calm down."

"You have no idea how difficult it's been seeing Michelle like that, knowing he was alive and not being able to tell her." Alyssa folded her arms and shivered at the breeze.

"I can imagine," Trevin said with understanding, putting his arm around her shoulders. "But he's back now."

"That bothers me even more." Alyssa turned into him. "I need to talk to him."

"Well, I suggest giving them some space first." The fear in her eyes made Trevin uneasy.

CHAPTER 2

Since Remus had left, Michelle had moved into the manor and gave the house she was living in to Trevin. Alyssa had been coming around a lot more, and it had become obvious why. She was a few months pregnant. They had gotten married soon after. Rubeus was unaware of the move when he brought Michelle back to the house.

"Did you redecorate?" Rubeus looked around the house, slightly confused.

"I don't live here anymore," Michelle replied from the doorway. He looked back at her. "I moved back into the manor since it became vacant and gave this to Trevin." The thought of Remus ran through his mind. It still hurt. "We don't have to stay there if it'll be too much for you."

"No, it'll be fine," Rubeus said with a hint of anxiety, taking one last look around before heading out. "But maybe we'll go somewhere else for a while."

"Don't you want to check in with the other elders?" Michelle asked.

"They've gotten by this long without me. They'll be fine for a few more days," Rubeus replied. "There's this really nice place I want to show you." He took her hand and disappeared with her. They reappeared inside a little cabin on the beach. There were no other homes around it, and it was almost hidden within the banana trees that lined the beach. Michelle stepped up to one of the windows that overlooked the beach and ocean.

"Where are we?"

"The beach," Rubeus answered.

"I know, but what realm?" Michelle looked back at him. "This doesn't look human, but it's too nice to be demonic."

"We're still in our realm," Rubeus informed her. "Just on the opposite coast. This place is new, though."

"It looks lived in." Michelle pulled herself from the window and looked around. They were standing in the living room. Everything was made of wicker. The kitchen was directly behind it, with a couple of stools setting behind a couch in front of the breakfast bar.

"I've never seen anyone," Rubeus stated as he went into the kitchen.

"How would you? You've been in a coma," Michelle responded. Rubeus straightened as he picked up something in the kitchen and threw it away.

"Yeah, I also said I was out of it for a month," Rubeus replied. Michelle sat on one of the stools and watched him. "What?" he asked when he finally looked over at her.

"Just thinking," Michelle said as she put her elbow on the countertop and propped her head up with her fist. "What did you do for that month awake?"

"I found this place and stayed here," Rubeus said, leaning across the kitchen table. "Until I felt well enough to come back."

"Let me get this straight—you woke from your coma, didn't have a lot of strength, so you traveled to the other side of the realm, which takes energy, to fully heal?" Michelle crossed her arms.

"You don't believe me?" Rubeus asked. He could tell by her tone and expression that she didn't. He held eye contact with her.

"It just doesn't make sense. But hey, if you say that's what you did, then that's what you did," Michelle said as she got up. "I mean, you wouldn't lie to me."

"You're right, I wouldn't," Rubeus said, knowing she knew he was. Michelle went outside. "Unless I was forced to." He followed her outside, but she wasn't on the porch. He saw her standing at the shoreline. "What's wrong?" Rubeus asked as he approached her.

"What's wrong? I thought you were dead, but you were in a coma," Michelle said, voice shaky. "Somebody had to have known. Somebody knew and didn't tell me. These past months would have been so much easier."

"I don't know what to tell you except I'm sorry."

"It's not your fault," Michelle said softly as she looked back to the ocean. "It's not like you could have told me."

"Well, I'm here now," Rubeus reassured her, pulling her into his arms. "And I don't plan on going anywhere."

She reached up and kissed him. "We have a lot of time to make up for." Michelle looked up at him.

"Yes, we do." Rubeus picked her up and started back towards the house.

"What's wrong with out here?" Michelle asked.

"Oh, don't worry, we'll make it out this way," Rubeus promised. They smiled at each other as he carried her inside.

CHAPTER 3

Alyssa was pacing back and forth in the kitchen with unrest.

"All this stress you're putting on yourself isn't healthy for you or the baby," Trevin stated.

"If I knew where they went, it wouldn't be so bad," Alyssa said, finally sitting down. "I really thought they would have just gone to the manor."

"Maybe they didn't because they knew you'd look," Trevin suggested. "They were apart for eight months. Let them have their time. It's not like they left for good."

"I'm going to see Nerissa," Alyssa said. She disappeared.

Since she was now the Apostle, Alyssa was able to travel directly inside the golden dome between the realms. She found there were a lot of short cuts she could take with the new position. She went straight to the castle.

"Good evening," Nerissa said as Alyssa walked into the study. "How are you feeling?" She nodded towards her abdomen.

"Fine," Alyssa said, slightly annoyed.

"You look stressed."

"Rubeus is back," Alyssa stated with concern in her

voice.

Nerissa stopped what she was doing. "Alive?" Nerissa asked under her breath. Alyssa didn't catch it. "What did he find out?"

"I don't know," Alyssa said, getting worked up again. "I haven't been able to talk to him. I don't even know where he is right now. He took off with Michelle a week ago."

"Well, that's to be expected," Nerissa responded with ease. "How did she take it?"

"He lied to her about where he was."

"Really?" Nerissa asked, surprised.

"Well, I sort of forced him to."

"The less they know about it, the better." Nerissa sat down and motioned for Alyssa to do the same. "So why are you so stressed over it?"

"Because I don't know what he found out," Alyssa complained. "If the destruction and reconstruction of the realms really opened a rift, we need to know. Especially if what comes out of it is a demon hunter. Their species depends on it."

"The other elders banished them all once we came to an agreement and created McCain," Nerissa replied. "There shouldn't be any left."

"Shouldn't be," Alyssa said, sitting down. "Doesn't mean there isn't."

"So what if a demon hunter comes out? It'll knock their population down a bit. They could use a good cleansing," Nerissa said.

"My best friend is a demon," Alyssa snapped. "The father of my unborn child is a demon."

"I can't help that you made poor choices," Nerissa said with a slightly raised tone.

"Why do you hate them so much?" Alyssa asked.

"Did you not see how they looked at our kind when they were here?" Nerissa questioned. "It's disgusting. I never would have let them here under any other circumstances."

"You created them," Alyssa reminded her.

"You haven't been around since the creation of the realms. I wouldn't expect you to understand."

"So if you don't care what comes out of that rift, why did you want Rubeus sent there to find out?" Alyssa asked. Nerissa didn't say anything at first. "You wanted it to kill him."

"It's not like everyone didn't already think that anyway. He at least would have severely injured it," Nerissa defended herself. "It could be a threat to our species too."

"You mean *your* species," Alyssa replied. "I stopped being just a witch when I took Remus's power. I'm responsible for both realms, so I need to know."

"Then go find out what he knows."

"I would if I knew where he was," Alyssa said with more annoyance. "Which is my original problem."

"You're the Apostle. You can locate anyone," Nerissa said as she pointed upstairs. "McCain spent most of his time up there. He was quite obsessed."

"That's what that orb up there is for?" Alyssa inquired, curious now. "It'll show me where anyone is?"

"It'll give you their coordinates," Nerissa said. "McCain knew the realms so well he could actually see where they were instead of the numbers. There's a map up there too."

Alyssa went up to the next level and into a tiny room off to the left. The room was dark, and in the center was a small round table with tall legs. A purple orb floated on top of it. A map of the human realm was on the left wall and the demonic on the right. As she approached the orb, it started to glow.

"Do I ask it or just think of the name?" Alyssa asked herself out loud. Smoke filled the orb, and numbers appeared. She looked for something to write on when a red dot on the demonic map appeared. Alyssa went over to the map. "Why is he on the other side of the realm?" She looked more closely and saw that there was a recent addition to the map. "That's where the rift is. Did he take Michelle there?" A second dot appeared, just about overlapping the first one. All of a sudden, both dots disappeared. Out of the corner of her eye, she saw two dots appear on the other side of the map.

***

"Where's Alyssa?" Michelle asked as Trevin walked into the alchemy lab. She was busy making potions. "You two have been glued to each other."

"She got tired of waiting for your return." Trevin sat down in one of the chairs by a bookshelf. "She went to see Nerissa."

"Why was she waiting?"

"She wants to talk to Rubeus." Trevin grabbed a book off the bookcase and flipped through it. "Where is he anyway?"

"Somewhere upstairs, I guess." Michelle shrugged. "What does she need to talk to him about?"

"She wouldn't say," Trevin said with uninterest. Michelle studied him and picked up on something.

"How is she doing otherwise?" Michelle asked, now more curious.

"She seems fine." Trevin shut the book and put it back. "We were going to keep it a secret, but it's pretty obvious now." Michelle looked away. "I know it's a sensitive subject for you. I'll try not to bring it up when you're around."

"Don't be silly. It's fine," Michelle said. "Really. I'm happy for you." They were both silent for a moment.

"Well, I'm gonna leave you to all this," Trevin said as he got up. "Feel free to make up some extras. I'm kinda low on everything."

"Having me make everything for you isn't helping you," Michelle replied.

"You sound just like Rubeus." Trevin shook his head as he left the lab and went to find his brother. Rubeus was in the dining room skimming over the volumes of books that lined the bookshelves against the wall. "Looking for something in particular?"

"I'm not sure what I'm looking for," Rubeus confessed, not looking up. "Congratulations, by the way."

"For what?" Trevin inquired. Rubeus looked over at him. "Oh, that." He shrugged it off. "I always thought it'd be you first. You were way more promiscuous than me."

Rubeus laughed as he pulled another book and sat at the table. "I almost was, more than once," Rubeus stated. "But nothing a little potion can't fix."

"What? You didn't," Trevin said in disbelief. "Even with Michelle?"

"No, not with her," Rubeus said. "I didn't need to."

"You're unbelievable," Trevin said with disgust.

"Don't get me wrong, it was disappointing with her, but I don't need or want a kid right now," Rubeus defended. "It's about time *you* had one."

"What's that supposed mean?" Trevin asked, getting heated. "It's about time for you too. You deserve multiples after what you just told me."

"You're three hundred years older than me," Rubeus

responded. "I'm still in double digits, a baby compared to you."

"Yeah, and you've had more partners than my existence," Trevin stated matter of factly.

"I have not," Rubeus snapped. "You're the reason I got that kind of reputation anyway." He slammed the book shut and put it back. They heard the front door open.

"Rubeus!" Alyssa called out. "I know you guys are back."

Rubeus let out a heavy sigh. "Why am *I* the one getting blasted with the pregnancy hormones?"

"Call it payback," Trevin replied. Rubeus shot him a look.

"You shouldn't be back," Alyssa stated as she found Rubeus and Trevin in the dining room, her tone and stance exuding dominance.

"I didn't find anything there, so I left," Rubeus replied, crossing his arms, not liking her threatening posture. "Maybe you could elaborate on what exactly I was searching for. You and Nerissa were vague with it."

"Can we discuss this somewhere else?" Alyssa asked. "I don't want Michelle to hear."

"Oh, but my brother can know?"

"She didn't willingly tell me," Trevin said, not wanting to get involved in what was about to happen. He could feel the tension radiating off both of them. "All I know is that you weren't really dead."

Alyssa went to grab Rubeus's arm, but he jerked away from her. "We're staying here," Rubeus said sternly as he put the table between them.

"No, we're not." Alyssa leaned over the table and grabbed for him again. He moved back, but she got a hold of his shirt. They started to disappear. Their energy swirled violently together and flickered in and out of existence as they fought for control of the teleport. Trevin had to shield his eyes from it. Rubeus pushed inside her mind and forced her thoughts out. They materialized back in the dining room with Alyssa screaming "get out" and putting her hands over her ears. Trevin rushed to her side as Rubeus stepped away. What he had seen was startling.

Michelle had heard all the commotion from the basement and was standing in the doorway, unnoticed.

"Why didn't you tell me that's why I was sent there?" Rubeus demanded.

Alyssa was still on the floor shaking. "If you knew the real reason, you wouldn't have gone," Alyssa said, looking up at him.

"I would have regardless if what you suspect is true," Rubeus said. "Demons need to know."

"You would cause a mass panic," Alyssa explained as Trevin moved her to one of the chairs.

"It's my job to keep them informed," Rubeus responded. "Their safety is my responsibility."

"Someone like to inform me of what may or may not be going on?" Michelle finally asked. Everyone looked over.

"This is something only the elders need to know right now," Alyssa said.

"I am an elder, in case you forgot," Michelle said with irritation. "And what about Trevin then?"

"Sleeping with the Apostle makes him special," Rubeus commented. Trevin glared over at him. Rubeus walked towards Michelle.

"Don't," Alyssa ordered.

"You need to learn your place. I don't take orders from

you," Rubeus said as he faced her. "You're not lord of the realms. You're a glorified peacekeeper. Your only job is to make sure the laws are upheld between the two realms and make sure justice is served if they aren't." Energy sparked to life around him. "McCain may have been a lot of things, but at least he kept his nose out of our affairs."

"The Apostle isn't just a peacekeeper," Alyssa said, standing. "You may rule over this realm, but I have to ensure the protection of everyone in both. And this poses a threat to yours. They'll kill her."

"They'll kill everyone!" Rubeus yelled at her as his eyes completely dilated and energy spun around him more violently. Alyssa and Trevin took a step back.

"They'll be more inclined to if —" Alyssa started.

"Stop talking," Trevin whispered sternly to her as he took her hand.

"…everyone panics." Alyssa finished anyway. "So you can't make it public."

"I'm not lying to her anymore!" Rubeus screamed. He pushed his arms forward, and a large magnitude of energy threw the table into the air. Trevin disappeared with Alyssa as it crashed into the wall, splintering into hundreds of pieces. Michelle put her hand on his shoulder. Rubeus turned around at the ready until he realized it was Michelle. She moved her hand to the side of his face and took some of the built-up energy he was holding into herself. Rubeus calmed down, and his eyes returned to normal. Michelle slowly gave what she had taken back. "I'm sorry," he whispered as he closed his eyes and leaned his head against hers. "I didn't want to lie to you." He wrapped his arms around her.

Moments later, Michelle stormed outside the manor.

"He attacked me!" Alyssa yelled at her, pointing inside

the manor.

"Law number one, don't provoke a daywalker," Michelle said in an unforgiving tone. "You provoked him! How could you keep this from me?!" She grabbed ahold of her throat, eyes slightly changing.

"How are you gonna be mad at *me*? He's the one that lied to you," Alyssa choked out.

"Against his will. You knew he was alive this *whole* time," Michelle said, malice in her voice. She thought about squeezing tighter but let her go instead, feeling betrayed. "I don't know why I'm surprised; you've been lying to me from the beginning."

Both were silent.

Alyssa finally sighed, breaking the silence. "It's not like I wanted to," Alyssa said, sitting down on the swinging bench.

"Well, now's your chance to confess," Michelle said, more calm but keeping her distance. "There should be no reason to keep anything from me anymore."

"You're not going to like it."

CHAPTER 4

The receptionist jumped out of her chair, startled, when she saw Rubeus enter City Hall. She looked at him like he was a ghost. She adjusted her glasses to make sure she was seeing straight.

"Good afternoon, Susan," Rubeus nodded, flashing her a smile. He went to the elevators behind her. "Be a dear and have the others meet me in my office in...I don't know, fifteen minutes?" He stepped into the elevator.

"Uh, yes, sir," Susan said, still in shock. The doors to the elevator closed. Susan picked up the phone on her desk and pushed a button. "Elder Camilla? You're not going to believe this."

***

"Nerissa has been watching over me ever since I was born," Alyssa started. "When I came of age to start understanding things, she told me I had an important role, and part of it was to watch over you until you turned eighteen." They were both staring at the wooden boards of the patio as they swayed the swinging bench with their feet.

"You knew what I was the entire time?" Michelle questioned, stopping the swing from moving as she looked over at Alyssa.

Alyssa nodded, seeing the hurt and distrust in Michelle's eyes. "She forbade me to say anything to you. She said it would mess up your destiny." Michelle stood and moved away from her. "She kept things from me too, like McCain being my father."

Michelle turned to say something, but her phone rang. She looked at it and shook her head before answering it.

"Why are you calling me from inside?" Michelle asked, voice slightly shaky.

"I'm at City Hall," Rubeus said on the other end. "I need to see you in my office."

"Right now?"

"Yes, I've called a meeting," Rubeus replied. "Five minutes." He hung up.

Michelle sighed, putting her phone away. "I apparently have to go. We'll continue this conversation later."

"He's summoning you back inside?" Alyssa asked with a disapproving tone.

"No, he's at City Hall and has called a meeting with the other elders."

"Well, maybe I should join you," Alyssa suggested as she stood up.

"I would let him be for a while," Trevin said from the doorway. "You don't ever want to see that side of him."

"Fine. I should go tell Nerissa what I found out anyway. I'll see you later." Alyssa disappeared.

"I've never seen him that angry," Michelle admitted.

"Well, I roughed him up a bit before Alyssa showed up," Trevin confessed.

"How?" Michelle asked.

Trevin shook his head. "Guy stuff," he finally answered.

Michelle rolled her eyes and shook her head before

disappearing.

***

Michelle walked into City Hall and was greeted by Susan.

"Do you know?" Susan asked as she stood up.

"Depends on what you're referring to," Michelle said, stopping in front of the desk. She picked up a stack of messages and sifted through them. Susan leaned forward.

"Rubeus is here," she whispered. "At least, I think it was him."

"It was really him," Michelle confirmed, pulling what was for her and setting the rest back on the desk, making eye contact with Susan. Michelle had always admired her emerald green eyes with flecks of yellow in them. They went well with her fire engine red hair. If only she would let it out of the tight bun she always wore, she would be quite stunning.

"That's great for you. How are you holding up?" Susan asked, adjusting her glasses.

"Fine. We spent last week together," Michelle said.

"How — ?" Susan started.

"Excuse me." Michelle interrupted, done talking about it.

She went to the elevator and took it up to the top floor. Michelle stepped out into a large open area and up a few steps that were several feet from the elevator. A few more feet, and she opened the door that led to Rubeus's office. She walked down the long hallway.

"When were you planning on telling us?" Camilla demanded.

"I'm telling you now," Rubeus said.

"Does Michelle know?" Sven inquired.

As if on cue, Michelle walked into the open area. The

other elders became quiet, waiting to see her reaction. She stopped as everyone stared at her.

"What?" Michelle asked. "You look like you've all seen a ghost." She walked up and stopped beside Rubeus. The others looked at each other.

"She knew. I've been back for a week." Rubeus sat down at his desk, rested his arms on it, and laced his fingers together.

"Where have you been then?" Arixanna questioned.

"I was sent to check a rift that opened after the destruction and regeneration of the realms," Rubeus explained.

"Rifts happen all the time," Sven replied. "Why is this one so important?"

"Nerissa and Alyssa weren't clear on the why," Rubeus admitted. "Just that it needed to be looked into. I couldn't find anything worth bringing back." Michelle gave him a questioning look since he didn't mention the realization he had back at his brother's place.

"Stupid witch business," Camilla mumbled. "Why did *you* need to be the one to do it?"

"Probably because it's in our realm," Rubeus said.

"If Nerissa's so concerned with it, she should check it out herself," Camilla responded, clearly angry over it.

"She's been between the realms for so long she's probably afraid to leave," Arixanna stated.

"She's starting a new civilization there," Rubeus added. "You should see it; it's crawling with them."

"You should try to get information from Alyssa," Camilla turned to Michelle.

"I was starting to, but then was summoned here," Michelle replied.

"She's been lying about who she is since the day you met her. Do you really think she's going to start telling you the truth now?" Rubeus asked.

"She doesn't have any reasons left to lie," Michelle answered.

"That you know of," Rubeus said.

"Where is the new rift?" Sven asked, changing the subject back to what mattered.

"The other side of the realm," Rubeus answered.

"Do you have a map?" Sven inquired.

"I wouldn't have a clue where one is." Rubeus started pulling open drawers at his desk. "Isn't there one hung up on the walls somewhere?"

Michelle stepped behind the desk and pulled open the top right drawer. She lifted some files up and pulled out a folded map. Rubeus looked at her questioningly.

"What?" Michelle asked. "You were dead. Someone had to take your place." She pushed everything off the desk to make room for the map. He gave her a small smile as she unfolded the map on it. Michelle knew it bothered him, which was partly why she did it. "This place was a mess—I reorganized it."

Rubeus looked around the open room and noticed that things weren't in the same places he remembered.

"It wasn't that bad in here," Rubeus said. "But I never had a chance to make it my own."

"What did you do for those first few months when I never saw you?" Michelle remarked, striking another nerve.

"I was hardly in here," Rubeus stated, annoyed. He looked at the map. "This is outdated."

"Nothing's changed in millennia," Camilla said. "Even during the regeneration. Everything is exactly the same."

"Are you sure about that?" Rubeus asked, looking up at them.

"Yes, we looked the place over while you were gone," Arixanna confirmed.

"Well, where I was isn't on here," Rubeus replied.

"Then maybe it wasn't our realm," Sven said, somewhat relieved.

"It's our realm," Rubeus confirmed. "I was past all this." He pointed to a heavily vegetative area right at the edge of the map. "There's a beach and ocean after this."

"Is that where you took me?" Michelle looked over at the map with new interest.

"Yeah," Rubeus said.

"Is there a cave?" Camilla questioned.

"Yes, but it's sealed off," Rubeus answered.

"I need to see the missing part," Camilla said.

"I wonder...," Michelle said, mainly to herself. She grabbed the drawer handle directly in front of Rubeus. He pushed back in the chair and gave her an annoyed look. She had barely waited for him to move out of the way before pulling it open.

"What are you looking for?" Rubeus asked as she searched for something with her hand in the drawer.

"I found a button a while back." Michelle continued feeling around for it. Rubeus leaned forward and pushed the drawer shut, almost clipping her hand. She shot him a look.

"This?" he asked as he pushed a button under the desk, not in the drawer. Part of the far wall opened. Sven, Camilla, and Arixanna turned and looked behind them, surprised.

"Hardly in here, huh?" Michelle commented as she moved from behind the desk to the secret entrance. Rubeus got up and followed her to it, the other elders close behind.

"I spent a lot of time here after you left," Rubeus said. The room was dark, cold, and damp. Rubeus ignited an orb of fire in his palm. It illuminated the room. There were books, scrolls, and rolled up parchment everywhere. Cobwebs and dust covered everything. An old rickety looking table was in the center of the room with a few alchemy supplies sitting on it. Michelle picked up a piece of parchment off the table, a recipe with no title. She quickly recognized it as the doppelganger recipe and dropped it as images flashed through her mind. She and Rubeus made eye contact as she moved away from it. An apologetic look formed on his face. Michelle looked away from him and turned to one of the bookcases. The other three elders were on the right side of the room looking at the other books and scrolls. They looked like kids in a candy store.

Rubeus flipped a beaker right side up on the table and put the fiery orb into it to free up his hand. Michelle had pulled a few maps off the bookcase. She sneezed as dust fell off them and into the air. There was a little desk off to the right that she started unrolling them on. They were all maps of different areas in the human realm. Michelle unrolled the last one she had grabbed.

"Hey, this is —," Michelle started as she turned to Rubeus. He wasn't there. She looked around and saw that everyone but Arixanna was no longer in the room. Michelle stuck her head out into the office and saw Sven and Camilla carrying an armload of books and scrolls into one of the rooms off to the left. Rubeus was over by his desk, picking stuff up off the floor that she had pushed off. Michelle went back into the room. All the maps had rolled back up into one large roll. She unrolled them again and picked up the top one. The rest rolled back up and off the table.

"Did   you   find   something?"   Arixanna   asked,

approaching her but keeping some distance. That night she had pinned Michelle to the wall was never spoken about, and they were never left alone since then.

"This is a map of the space between the realms," Michelle said, studying it. Their shoulders brushed, and Michelle tensed as Arixanna came close enough to see the map. It didn't go unnoticed, as Michelle took a step away.

"Perhaps we should talk about it," Arixanna said, facing her.

"There's nothing to talk about," Michelle stated, trying to focus on the map. "It was a misunderstanding."

"Well, I can't express how sorry I am." Arixanna reached for her but hesitated.

"Don't be. It was my fault," Michelle said. "I didn't know I was doing it, and I couldn't control it at the time." The maps that had rolled onto the floor hit her foot as they both felt a small breeze. They both looked at the wall between the bookcase and table.

"I'll get Rubeus," Arixanna said.

"Don't. He's busy having an OCD moment," Michelle said, laying down the map she had.

"A what?" Arixanna asked, confused.

Michelle smiled lightly and shook her head as she went to get the orb of fire. Arixanna grabbed her wrist.

"You can't touch someone else's energy," Arixanna said sternly. "It'll hurt you."

"I can touch his," Michelle informed her.

Rubeus went to the other side of his desk and opened the top right drawer. He lifted the files and folders to put the map back and stopped when he saw a wallet-sized picture. He picked it up after returning the map. It was a picture of a man and woman with their son. The son appeared to be about his age—Rubeus recognized him as Trevin. He sat down as he looked at the picture. Rubeus had never known what his parents looked like since they were both killed at the time of his birth, and Remus never had any photos hanging around the manor. The man almost looked identical to him.

He suddenly felt a small shift in his energy and looked over at the hidden room, where he saw Michelle with the orb of fire he had created. He put the picture in the bottom left corner of the frame, which held a picture of Michelle and him on their wedding day, on his desk and got up. He went back to the hidden room as Michelle and Arixanna were checking out where the breeze came from.

"Find something?" Rubeus asked.

Michelle was kneeling by the bookcase with the orb looking for anything that showed signs of another hidden entrance. "I found a map of the space between the realms," Michelle said, flicking her hand towards the table. "And I think there's another hidden entrance in here. We felt a breeze."

Rubeus looked at the map. "Not much to it," Rubeus replied, uninterested.

Michelle started to push on the bookcase but to no avail. It was too heavy for her to move.

"Watch out." Michelle moved out of the way as Rubeus effortlessly moved it a few feet to the left. There was a brick a little brighter than the rest, and it wasn't seated in concrete like the others were. Michelle pulled the brick out and held the orb up to the hole.

"I can't see anything," Michelle said, on her tiptoes.

Rubeus stuck his hand in the hole and felt around. He pushed in deeper until he was up to his shoulder, and the side of his face was pressed up against the wall. His hand came out on the other side up to his elbow, and he grabbed ahold of something. It felt like a lever. Rubeus pulled it towards himself. Gears cranking sounded as he brought his arm back out, pulling cobwebs off his hand.

"What did you do?"

He shrugged his shoulders as they waited for something to happen. The wall started to rumble as dust fell. Rubeus pushed Michelle and Arixanna back as Michelle put a bubble around them. The section of the wall that the bookcase was in front of pushed back a few inches before sliding to the right.

"How is there room for this on the top floor?" Arixanna asked, amazed, as Michelle lowered the shield. There was a staircase that went down.

"Because it's a portal, and this is just reflecting what's there," Rubeus stated.

"How do you know that?" Michelle asked, slightly accusingly.

"This staircase is in the castle," Rubeus said.

"Well, how do you know what the staircases there look like?" Michelle questioned.

"That's where I was taken after my death," Rubeus replied. "I did some exploring before heading off to investigate the rift."

"I'll go let the other two know what we found," Arixanna said, not wanting to be part of whatever was about to happen next between them. She left the room.

"Shall we?" Rubeus asked, offering his arm.

"I don't know," Michelle said with a hint of anger, crossing her arms. "What else are you keeping from me?"

"Nothing," Rubeus answered. "You're not seriously getting mad *now*, are you?"

"I've been mad," Michelle replied. "You lied to me.

And what's worse is, you knew that I knew you were lying, and you still did it."

"It's not like I wanted to," Rubeus responded. "I've already explained all this to you."

"You could've popped in real quick and been like, 'Hey, I'm alive and well, but I gotta go do this other thing over here,'" Michelle said.

"You would've wanted to come with me," Rubeus said.

"You're damn right I would have," Michelle snapped.

"I had to do it by myself," Rubeus explained. "I didn't know what I was looking for or what I might find. I couldn't chance putting you in that kind of danger."

"I don't need your constant protection." Michelle stepped back from him as he went to reach for her. Rubeus stopped and lowered his hand with a hurt expression as she put a shield up. He looked away from her and at the portal.

"You're right," Rubeus confessed.

"Excuse me?" Michelle asked, dropping the shield.

"I should have come by and told you instead of letting you think I was dead," Rubeus said solemnly. "And I know you're perfectly capable of handling yourself. I trained you."

"And you did a fine job." Michelle stepped up to him. "So good, in fact, that I can stand up to *you*, the one everyone is afraid of."

"You're the only one who could do it and win," Rubeus admitted as he looked back over at her. She wrapped her arms around him. "Are we good?"

"We're good," Michelle said. She reached up and kissed him. "Until you do something else that's stupid." He playfully pushed her away from him. "Come on. Let's go give Nerissa a visit." Rubeus took her offered hand, and they went through the portal.

CHAPTER 5

"You're positive he found nothing?" Nerissa asked as she turned away from one of the windows in the castle hallway.

"That's what he said," Alyssa reiterated.

"He's gotta be lying." Nerissa started walking down the hall. "Or he didn't look hard enough."

"He was searching for months," Alyssa replied.

"Maybe if you told me I was supposed to be looking for demon hunters, I would have been more successful," Rubeus commented.

Nerissa froze at the sound of his voice. She turned around and saw Rubeus and Michelle.

"How did you get here?" Nerissa asked, surprised. "I made this place impossible for demons to get to. Even after being here."

"We found a portal in my office," Rubeus answered.

"Bane said he got rid of it." Nerissa scowled under her breath as she looked away. "Well, what do you want?"

"Information would be nice," Michelle said, stepping forward.

"I'm actually kind of interested in why Bane had a portal to here, to begin with," Rubeus said with curiosity.

Nerissa's face flushed as she quickly turned away from them.

"You and Bane?" Michelle asked, shocked.

"It was a long time ago," Nerissa explained. "Witches are always born female, so we needed a way to carry on our species, which is the real reason why we created you. We engineered your species to be predominately male, but things got out of control."

"Must have been a flaw in your design," Rubeus roused.

Nerissa glared over at him. "There was no flaw," Nerissa snapped as she stepped towards them but still keeping her distance. "Your kind became power hungry."

"I think everyone knows the history," Alyssa said in an attempt to break the rising hostility. "Let's talk about this demon hunter."

"I've nothing to share about them." Nerissa turned and started to leave. A blue field went up in front of her.

"We're not leaving until you do share with us," Michelle said as Nerissa turned around. Michelle was standing in front of her. Nerissa's heart skipped a beat, and her golden eyes widened as she tried to move away. Michelle grabbed her wrist, and Nerissa froze, a hint of fear in her eyes. "Tell us what you know about them."

"The name is pretty explanatory," Nerissa said as she pulled out of her grip and moved away from Michelle's reach.

"How can we find them?" Michelle questioned.

"You needn't worry about that," Nerissa stated. "They'll find you."

"You created them, didn't you?" Rubeus asked. "You should be able to tell us something."

"That doesn't mean I know everything there is to know

about them," Nerissa replied. "But I may know someone who can help you."

"Who?" Michelle asked.

"I'll need a couple days to find her," Nerissa answered. "I'll give Alyssa the information when I have it." She flicked her hand at Michelle and Rubeus, and an orb flew out and hit them, causing them to disappear.

Alyssa looked over at Nerissa. "You act like they have the plague," Alyssa said. "Like their touch is deadly."

"They might as well be," Nerissa responded. "If they knew the full truth, we'd all be in danger." She disappeared down the hall.

CHAPTER 6

"Did you see how she looked at us?" Michelle asked from the living room in the manor.

"She hates our existence." Rubeus shrugged. "The humans give us the same look. Why do you let it bother you so much?"

"You didn't grow up as or think you were a human your whole life," Michelle stated. "You can't understand—"

"I'm gonna stop you right there before you get yourself in too deep." Rubeus looked over at her as Michelle gave him a questioning look. "Remember when we first officially met?"

"Of course."

"You thought I was human, remember?" Rubeus asked. "Even knowing you didn't know, I still went out of my way to make sure you made it home safely."

"Yeah, but—" Michelle started.

Rubeus held his hand up to stop her. "Now, remember the next time we ran into each other?" Rubeus asked. Michelle nodded. "And how your attitude suddenly changed towards me when you found out I was a demon?" Michelle said nothing. "Don't act like you're so appalled by the prejudice of others when you were guilty of it too."

"I was wrong for that. But in my defense, you were

stalking me," Michelle replied.

"I wasn't stalking you," Rubeus laughed. "I was...."
He thought a moment. "Huh, I guess I was. But I had good
reason."

"Sure." Michelle smiled. "If turning my life upside is a
good reason."

"You're happy, aren't you?" Rubeus inquired.

"I am, but before this gets even farther off course, back
to Nerissa," Michelle said. "When I grabbed ahold of her, I
sensed fear." Rubeus looked over at her. "She's afraid of our
touch. I intend to find out why."

CHAPTER 7

"I practically gift wrap you a pureblood, and you can't even get out of bed to dispose of him," Nerissa said as she entered the cave. It was pitch black inside. Two glowing yellow eyes appeared several feet in front of her.

"You should've told me I was going to have company," the demon hunter responded in a deep voice. "I guess I'll have to settle for you."

Nerissa shimmered in and out of existence as he tried to grab ahold of her. She laughed. "You actually think I'm stupid enough to physically come to you?"

"What do you want, Nerissa?" the demon hunter sighed.

"I need you to go to the human realm and find this woman." Nerissa held a picture up.

"Why would I want to do that?"

"Because I'm sending the demons to her," Nerissa replied. "Her brother has a very special talent that they're going to need. If you intercept them and activate his true purpose, it'll work to your advantage."

"If you want to be rid of them so badly, why did you even create purebloods again?" the demon hunter inquired.

"I didn't create them again," Nerissa snapped. "The

other witch elders have perished, along with the spells we all cast on their species. I only allowed them to live so they could keep the realms from falling apart. Their existence is no longer needed."

"So that's how I've been released," the demon hunter thought out loud.

"Will you do it?" Nerissa asked.

The sound of wings echoed along the walls.

"I'll rid you of your pureblood problem, but then I'm coming for you," he threatened as he took off out of the cave.

"You won't live long enough to make it to me," Nerissa said as she watched him blink out.

CHAPTER 8

Michelle walked into the baby's room and saw Trevin sitting on the floor, looking at the directions to assemble the crib.

"Do you know what she's going to be yet?" Michelle asked.

"Probably Alyssa's successor," Trevin said without looking up. "She should have both sides."

Rubeus was on his way up to talk to Trevin. He stopped and leaned against the doorframe when he saw Michelle in there.

"Don't get your hopes up. Rubeus isn't going to want one anytime soon. He's dodged it more times than you know."

"That's fine. I'm still young. I don't need to be tied down to one just yet," Michelle replied. "He doesn't seem like the settling type anyway."

"That's not entirely true," Trevin said, still not noticing his brother. "He settled for you." Michelle shot him a look. "That came out wrong."

Rubeus laughed in the doorway as he bit into an apple he had. They looked over at him.

"Horrible phrasing of words," Rubeus chuckled.

"How long have you been standing there?" Trevin

asked. Michelle looked away.

"Long enough to hear you tell her I kill babies," Rubeus replied.

"I didn't say you kill babies," Trevin retorted.

"Might as well have," Rubeus commented, biting into the apple again.

"I don't think you kill babies," Michelle reassured him as she looked back over. She felt the tension between them. "Should I?"

"No." Rubeus didn't take his eyes away from Trevin.

"Just unborn ones," Trevin let slip out. Rubeus's eyes started to dilate.

"So, my miscarriage wasn't an accident?" Michelle asked, a sickening feeling washing over her. His eyes went back to normal as he looked over at her.

"That *was* an accident," Rubeus said defensively. "Bane caused it, not me."

"But you knew right away."

"I knew," Rubeus repeated.

"And you let me think I was for three months?" Michelle accused, tears starting to form.

"Would you have believed me or a doctor?" Rubeus replied.

"That's not the point," Michelle snapped.

"It doesn't matter. You just said you didn't want one anytime soon," Rubeus said. "Neither do I."

"And what happens if I accidentally become pregnant again?" Michelle asked, walking up to him. She stopped beside him in the doorway.

"That won't happen," Rubeus said with confidence, looking at the apple as he brought it back up.

She shoved the apple into his mouth.

"You can't control that."

Michelle brought her knee up between his legs. He closed his eyes as the apple muffled his cry. She took the apple and left the room. Rubeus slid down to his knees, leaned forward onto his forearms, and let out a frustrated scream.

"Why would you even say anything to her about it?" Rubeus demanded angrily.

Trevin started to back up as Rubeus leapt for him. They wrestled around on the floor until Rubeus had him pinned on his back. He punched him first in the eye and then again on the side of his face before Trevin was able to get his arms up to block.

"Cut it out! Get off me!" Trevin yelled.

Alyssa ran into the room. "What are you guys doing?" Alyssa asked.

Michelle came back to the doorway and put her hand out. A shield materialized between them, pushing Rubeus off Trevin a few inches. As soon as Trevin rolled out and away from him, she let the shield vanish. Neither one of them said anything. Alyssa looked back at Michelle.

"Don't look at me," Michelle said, biting into the apple.

"I got that contact information," Alyssa stated. "We should go check it out tonight."

"I'm not going anywhere with any of you," Rubeus snapped, as he watched a cut on his fist close. Trevin glanced over. Rubeus looked at Trevin's face, confirming to them both.

"Well, that makes two of us," Trevin added. They glared at each other.

"I don't know what's going on with you two, and I don't much care, but this is going to happen," Alyssa said sternly.

"Not tonight, it isn't," Rubeus responded, leaving the

room. He snatched the apple back from Michelle, making her jump, and continued down the hall.

"What's *his* problem?" Alyssa asked.

"I'll tell you later," Michelle answered as they went downstairs. Michelle went to the kitchen and grabbed a dishtowel as Alyssa got some ice. She handed the towel wrapped ice to Trevin.

"Feel free to stay here for a few days," Trevin offered as he put the ice to his already bruised eye.

"What for?" Michelle inquired.

"I certainly wouldn't want to be around him after all that," Trevin admitted.

"I'm not afraid of him. Besides, he's mad at you, not me," Michelle replied.

"Do you ever try to fight him back?" Alyssa asked him.

"Are you crazy? You saw what happened to McCain," Trevin stated. "Besides, he can heal. You'd never be able to tell if I connected."

"I forgot about his blood being toxic," Alyssa said.

"At least it would be a quick death," Michelle added.

Trevin looked over at her and shook his head. "McCain died quickly because he injected it into his bloodstream. Any other form of contact will cause a much more painful death. I've seen that only once."

"What happened?" Alyssa asked.

The three sat down at the dining room table. Trevin put the ice down. The swelling had gone down a little, but his eye had already swollen shut.

"When he was little, he got in a fight at school," Trevin continued. "The other kid split his lip and broke his nose. Some of Rubeus's blood got in the kid's mouth, and he immediately started to seize up. He was rushed to the hospital, but there was no hope of saving him. They said it attacked his organs, shutting them down, and then hit every system. It completely dissolves you from the inside out until there's nothing left but this gelatinous goo."

"You're lying," Michelle said, not believing a word as she pushed away from the table.

"Ask him," Trevin dared. He put the ice back on his eye. "Ever since then, he did nothing but train so it would never happen again. No one can beat him. The only way you can connect is if he's distracted."

"I've seen him get hit before," Michelle stated.

"You're a distraction," Trevin replied. "He'd do anything to keep you from getting hurt."

"How do you deal?" Alyssa asked.

"Easy. Don't make him bleed," Trevin said.

"I find it hard to believe that someone would try to fight him," Michelle stated. "Regardless of how old he was."

"He got picked on a lot because he was different. He was the only pureblood at the time, and everyone was jealous."

"That's no reason," Michelle said disapprovingly.

"It's not, but everyone would look at him and see someone that the rules didn't apply to," Trevin added. "He didn't want to get into fights and avoided them as much as he could because of what could happen if he got injured. Fighting terrified him — it still does."

***

Michelle quietly entered the manor. She didn't know where Rubeus was inside if he went back there at all, but she really didn't want to run into him at the moment. Michelle tiptoed through the house, quietly checking different rooms. She eventually found him passed out on the couch in one of the living rooms with the TV on. She took a blanket, covered him, and turned the TV off before disappearing.

CHAPTER 9

Michelle materialized in the human realm just outside the mansion. No one was sure if Celeste was killed. Her body wasn't found, so everyone assumed she wasn't. Celeste hadn't been back to the mansion, from what Michelle could tell. After Remus had sacrificed his energy to Alyssa, she had put him up in the mansion so he wouldn't end up becoming a familiar if he stayed in the demonic realm. His energy stripped, he was able to be in the sunlight.

Even though the mansion was hers, she still felt she needed to knock since she no longer stayed there. Remus opened the door shortly after.

"You don't need to knock," Remus said as he let her in.

"I know." Michelle stepped inside as he shut the door. "You look well. How are you holding up?"

"It took some getting used to, but I'm managing it well enough," Remus said. "How can I help you?"

"Can't I just visit you?" Michelle turned to face him. Remus just looked at her, and Michelle sighed. "Okay, I have a dilemma, but I really did want to see how you were doing."

"It's appreciated," Remus said, walking into the living room. Michelle sat down on the couch, and Remus sat on the loveseat. The furniture was positioned facing each other, with a coffee table between them. A fireplace was off to Michelle's left, Remus's right. It was beginning to get cold in the human realm, so he had the fireplace on. "So, what's new?"

"I don't know if you've heard, but Rubeus is alive," Michelle started.

"He survived?" Remus asked, somewhat surprised.

"Yeah, Nerissa and Alyssa sent him to investigate a rift that opened up after the realms regenerated," Michelle explained. "He was gone for eight months."

"Rifts open all the time," Remus stated.

"That's what Sven said too."

"I'm sure Nerissa didn't indulge in the why," Remus remarked.

"She knows something and won't share it with us," Michelle said, not wanting to worry him with it. "But that's not what I came to talk to you about."

"What's Rubeus done now?"

"What makes you think it's about him?" Michelle asked.

"Because I know firsthand he isn't easy to live with," Remus responded. "He's stubborn and won't listen to reason, although he's gotten a lot better with that."

"I don't know much about his past," Michelle said, although she had a little deeper insight after Trevin's story. "Except for Bane killing his parents and something that happened between him and McCain."

"Those are really the only significant events that have happened," Remus said. "I didn't keep him sheltered, but I tried to keep him from getting into too much trouble. What exactly are you looking to know?"

"Trevin gave me the impression that he's lived a very active lifestyle in certain respects," Michelle answered. "And he has this big thing against having kids and has stopped several from happening."

"Well, your first problem is listening to anything Trevin has to say about Rubeus," Remus replied. "He exaggerates and is in constant competition with him. If he can make himself come out looking better than him, he will."

"Rubeus didn't disagree," Michelle added. "He didn't want me to know."

"I didn't involve myself with his sexual escapades," Remus stated. "I didn't want to know, but there were a couple times he came to me about an unexpected pregnancy. I told him the options he had and what could be done about it. How he acted is his business. You don't think he had something to do with *your* termination, do you?"

"No," Michelle said softly as she looked over at the fireplace. "But he admitted to knowing before I did."

"Well, all I can tell you is don't listen to Trevin and that it only happened twice," Remus reassured her. "He may have had a licentious reputation, but according to him, it was all hearsay."

"That makes me feel a little better."

"You're both young, so I can understand why he doesn't want any kids yet. Demons typically don't start having children until they're several hundred years old." Remus leaned forward and patted her leg. "If it bothers you that much, talk to him about it." Michelle laughed lightly. "Easier said than done, I know."

"I'm mad at him right now," Michelle stated.

"Use that." Remus smiled. "Nothing's worse to him than you being upset with him. You should have seen him when you left after the incident with Laura." Remus got up.

"Was it bad?" Michelle asked, following him into the

kitchen.

"You have no idea." Remus opened the fridge as Michelle leaned on the counter.

"So what about a fight he got into when he was younger?" Michelle asked. "Trevin told me about a kid that died from coming in contact with his blood."

Remus shut the door and faced her. "That story is true."

"Even down to what his blood does?" Michelle inquired.

"Yes." Remus nodded. "Rubeus was never one to fight growing up."

"I can see why," Michelle said. "He's terrifying when he does."

"He defuses it as quickly as possible, by any means necessary," Remus added. "Let's go out for dinner."

"That'd be nice," Michelle said. "Just us? Or do you want me to go get Rubeus?"

"If you want answers, stay mad at him," Remus said, answering her question indirectly.

"You and me it is."

They left the mansion.

CHAPTER 11

"What do you think you're doing?" Michelle pushed Rubeus away and turned on the lamp on the nightstand.

"What do you think?" he asked as he reached out again.

"Oh no, and chance getting pregnant? I don't think so," Michelle said as she got out of bed. "We're not having sex until you accept the fact that it's a possibility that you can't control. Or until you're ready to have one, whichever comes first. In your case, that may be forever."

"You can't do that," Rubeus snapped.

"I can, and I will."

"What am I supposed to do?" Rubeus folded his arms across his chest.

"You have two hands," Michelle replied. He scoffed at her comment, clearly insulted. "The spare is that way." She pointed towards the door.

"You can't be serious." Rubeus got out of bed.

"Oh, I'm sorry, I almost forgot," Michelle said as she went into the bathroom. "You'll need this." She tossed lotion and a box of tissues onto the bed.

He looked down at them. "I'm not taking that." Rubeus looked back up at her.

"It's your preference." Michelle turned away from him.

"You know you really can't say no. I've claimed you." Rubeus stood his ground.

Michelle gasped.

Rubeus closed his eyes and sighed. "Shit," he said under his breath as he realized what he had just said sounded like. "I didn't mean—"

"You have five seconds to get out of my sight." Michelle's eyes dilated as she turned to face him.

"Or what?" He looked over at her and faltered. Rubeus had never seen her eyes turn before. Even the whites of her eyes had turned black. Flames started to spark to life around her as her hair floated about her.

"Or you're going to see just how bad *my* temper can be," Michelle threatened. "Your five seconds are up."

Rubeus barely made it out of the manor before flames erupted through every door and window. He dove down the steps to the wraparound balcony to avoid the fire. He propped himself up on his elbows and looked up at the manor as the flames went out.

"Are you all right? The whole realm lit up," Trevin said as he appeared beside him.

"It's nothing." Rubeus stood as Michelle came to the front door, back to her normal self, and threw the lotion at him. He picked it up and threw it beside the door frame as she turned to go back in. It splattered everywhere.

She stopped and teleported in front of him. "Are you *trying* to make things worse?" Michelle loomed as she pushed him back. He grabbed ahold of her shirt and formed energy in his other hand. "I dare you," Michelle challenged. They stared at each other a moment longer before he let out a frustrated scream, then let her go and disappeared.

Trevin gave her a questioning look.

"I said no." She turned and went back inside the manor.

CHAPTER 12

Rubeus appeared in the human realm near the mansion, unaware Remus was alive and staying there when he went inside. As he went through the different rooms, Rubeus started noticing that someone was living there. His thoughts first went to Celeste since no one knew what had happened to her, but he didn't think she would continue staying there if she were still alive. Rubeus heard someone behind him and quickly turned and grabbed hold of the wrist that was preparing to strike him.

"Remus?" Rubeus asked, stunned, letting him go. "You're alive?"

"Yes, as are you." Remus rubbed his wrist. "What are you doing here?"

"I could ask *you* the same thing."

"Michelle's letting me stay here for the remainder of my time," Remus said, moving past him down the hall.

"Of course she knew about it," Rubeus muttered under his breath.

"Do I detect a hint of disdain towards her?" Remus asked.

"No," Rubeus responded. "We had a disagreement, which is why I came here. I needed to get away."

"Let me guess—you spoke before thinking," Remus replied as he went into another room and sat down.

"What makes you think it was me?" Rubeus asked in defense, following him.

"Because it's always you and your mouth. You have no filter," Remus answered. "She was here the other day asking about your past."

"Why?" Rubeus asked. "If she wants to know something, all she needs to do is ask."

"Perhaps you made her feel she couldn't."

"What was she asking about?" Rubeus inquired.

"Kids," Remus replied.

"This is all Trevin's fault." Rubeus rolled his eyes. "He's having one with Alyssa."

"Really? I wasn't aware of that," Remus pondered. "I guess that's what prompted it then. So tell me about this mission you were sent on while everyone thought you were dead."

"Nerissa wanted me to investigate a rift that opened on the west side of the realm."

"The west side has been closed off for millennia."

"Not anymore," Rubeus informed him. "The destruction and reconstruction of the realms must have opened it back up. She's convinced a demon hunter is loose."

"If that's true, be careful," Remus warned. "Their main purpose is to kill purebloods."

"I know," Rubeus assured him. "We're waiting to hear back from her with a contact that has information on them."

"That's ridiculous. Nerissa created them," Remus said with fervor.

"She claims to not know much about them."

"She knows more than she lets on," Remus replied. "If

she created it, she can destroy it. Be careful around her. She's the only one who can kill you."

"Not if I get to her first," Rubeus replied.

"She can pull that enzyme from you in a heartbeat," Dr. Lewis said as he entered the room. Rubeus looked over as Remus looked at his watch. Neither one of them heard him come in. "I wasn't aware you were going to have company. I can come back later if you want."

"No, it's fine," Remus said, slightly annoyed.

"You're that sick?" Rubeus asked with worry.

"Well, that's just it. I'm not," Remus said. "My power being taken from me took what was ailing me away too."

"I've been running tests on his blood every month to see if it's come back," Dr. Lewis added. "He still doesn't have a lot of time left, though."

"Why not?" Rubeus asked. "If you're no longer sick —"

"Because I'm human," Remus interrupted. "Their life span is only a fraction of ours. I've been around for two millennia; every day could be my last."

"Demons don't die from old age like humans do. Our systems don't shut down," Dr. Lewis explained. "Our power is what ultimately does us in. It changes and corrupts and starts to tear us apart from the inside."

"So what's going to happen to Alyssa? She has his power," Rubeus said.

"It's a new body, so it starts over," Dr. Lewis stated. "Unfortunately," he mumbled.

"Don't like her?" Rubeus asked.

"I don't care if she's the new Apostle. She was a witch first," Dr. Lewis said. "To think one of my own laid with her disgusts me."

Remus shot him a look.

"One of your own?" Rubeus looked at Dr. Lewis suspiciously. "I thought Trevin's dad died." He looked to Remus.

"I'm not his father. *His* father only wanted to procreate," Dr. Lewis replied. "He didn't love your mother like I did, but I raised him as my own."

"So...you're —" Rubeus started.

"I am *your* father," Dr. Lewis stated. "The first daywalker to be born in millennia."

"How is that possible?" Rubeus asked in disbelief. "Bane killed you."

"I wasn't there during his massacre," Dr. Lewis explained. "I was working late when Remus came into my office with you."

Rubeus looked over at Remus. "You've lied to me this whole time."

"I did it to protect you both," Remus responded. "Bane didn't know you survived, and he couldn't find your father. I had him change his name and appearance to protect him. I told him to stay away from you so Bane wouldn't make the connection. I couldn't let him find out. By the time he realized you had survived, killing you was out of his hands."

Rubeus stood up and paced around the room as he ran his hands through his hair. "I just...I can't believe all this."

"Well, you're handling it well," Dr. Lewis commented.

"I have so much on my mind right now I can't even process all this," Rubeus admitted. "I came here in hopes of having a quiet night, just to find out you're not dead," he said, looking at Remus. "...and you were never dead." He looked to Dr. Lewis. "What's your real name? Is Timmons even right?"

"Yes, I made sure you had my name." Dr. Lewis sat his bag down on a nearby table and pulled a necklace out from under his shirt. It had a charm on it. "I can't remember the last time I've taken this off." He looked at it for a moment before removing it. Energy swirled around him as his appearance changed. His hair was now the shade of garnet with yellow tips, and his eyes were purple. Rubeus was almost identical to him, except slightly taller and more tone. "Ryan is my real name." He held his hand out. Rubeus took it, and they shook hands.

"So does Michelle know about this too?" Rubeus inquired.

"No," Ryan answered questioningly. "Why would she?"

"She apparently knows everything else," Rubeus replied.

"He's having trouble in paradise," Remus informed. Rubeus shot him a look.

"Oh, so that's why you're here. She kicked you out," Ryan said.

"She didn't kick me out. I chose to leave."

"What was your other option?" Ryan asked.

"There wasn't one," Rubeus said.

"You could've apologized for whatever you did?" Remus suggested.

"She tried to catch me on fire," Rubeus snapped. "I'm not apologizing."

"That sounds more like something you would do," Remus replied.

"You should've seen her." Rubeus pictured her eyes. "And you think my temper is bad." He shook his head. "She lit the whole place up."

"Females *are* more powerful," Ryan stated. "What set her off?"

"I'd rather not get into that right now," Rubeus said, slightly embarrassed.

Ryan shrugged his shoulders as he opened his bag. "Shall we get to it then?" Remus offered his arm, and Ryan prepped it. He drew some blood and examined it. "You're still clean." Remus got up to make a drink. "Would you like to see what your blood does to others?"

"No thanks," Rubeus said, a little uneasy. "I've seen it more times than I'd care to."

"Either of you hungry?" Remus asked.

"I could eat," Ryan said, looking at his watch. "But it'll have to be quick. My next appointment is at two."

"Rubeus?" Remus queried.

"I guess," he said. "I haven't been out in this realm for a while. I should probably remind everyone I'm still around." Remus rolled his eyes and shook his head. "What?"

"Nothing," Remus said. "Let's go."

CHAPTER 13

"Where have *you* been the past couple of days?" Trevin interrogated as he sat down beside Rubeus in the living room at the manor.

"With Remus," Rubeus replied while flipping through a magazine. "Thanks for telling me, by the way."

"Sorry, I figured Michelle would have told you."

"I guess it slipped her mind." Rubeus tossed the magazine on the coffee table and glanced over at his brother. "Did you know about my father?"

"Everyone knows what happened to him," Trevin responded. "You know that."

"He's alive," Rubeus stated.

"Sure he is," Trevin said. "Mom is too, right here." He put his hand over his heart.

"I'm serious," Rubeus said, turning completely to face Trevin.

"And you're seriously starting to worry me." Trevin reached to put his hand on Rubeus's forehead. "Bane killed him."

"He wasn't there when it happened." Rubeus slapped Trevin's hand away and stood. "It's Dr. Lewis."

"Dr. Lewis is not your dad," Trevin said with confidence

as Rubeus moved past him.

"Remus had him disguise himself and change his name," Rubeus explained. "His real name is Ryan, and I look just like him." Trevin was silent. Rubeus turned to face him. "Did you know about it?"

"What? No," Trevin said defensively, coming to his feet.

"Don't lie to me about this." Rubeus stepped up to him in a challenging way.

"I'm not," Trevin said sternly, standing his ground. "That's not something I would keep from you."

"Unless you were told to," Rubeus replied.

"I swear I had no idea," Trevin said, changing his tone to something softer. "He's really alive?"

"Yeah," Rubeus answered, turning away from him.

"How did you take it?" Trevin questioned.

"Surprisingly well."

"You didn't even get a little upset?" Trevin asked.

"More so with Remus. But there are more important things to worry about right now," Rubeus said.

"Look at you. Growing up," Trevin said with a smile.

"I know, it's scary." Rubeus smiled back. "We need to go see Nerissa's contact."

Trevin's phone went off. "Yeah, that might have to wait," Trevin said, looking at the message. "Alyssa just went into labor. She's at the hospital with Michelle."

CHAPTER 14

Trevin was pacing back and forth in the waiting room at labor and delivery. They were in a human hospital since Alyssa was primarily a witch. The demonic realm wasn't able to service her needs.

"Sit down already," Rubeus said with annoyance. "You're starting to make even me nervous."

"I can't," Trevin said with concern. "It's been too long."

"Giving birth isn't a quick process," Michelle stated from the other side of the waiting room. She was watching a few storm clouds move in. "She could be in labor for a few hours to a few days."

"A few days?" Trevin asked, eyes wide.

"Yes," Michelle replied as she looked over at them. She made eye contact with Rubeus for a brief second before looking away again.

"I'm going to the cafeteria. Want anything?" Rubeus asked, wanting to get away from Michelle's iciness.

"No thanks," Trevin said softly.

"Text me if I'm not back in time," Rubeus said. Trevin nodded.

Rubeus left the waiting room without saying a word to Michelle. Trevin finally sat down.

"I can't believe you two are still fighting," Trevin said in an attempt to take his mind off everything else. "It couldn't have *just* been over sex."

Michelle looked back over at him. "Well, it was," she snapped, folding her arms.

"He wouldn't get mad over that," Trevin said.

Michelle spun towards him with anger in her voice. "Tell me I can't say no because you've claimed me and see what happens."

"Oh damn, he tried to use that against you?" Trevin asked.

"He didn't mean it the way it sounded, but he still shouldn't have said it," Michelle said more calmly. "And you're right. It's not the only reason. He thinks he can control everything, and he can't. You can't just decide to have kids whenever you want—it doesn't work that way. It's going to be unexpected, and you're never ready for it. He needs to grow up more anyway." She moved back to the window.

"He's done more of that in the past couple of days than you know," Trevin responded. They were both silent for a moment.

"She's going to be fine," Michelle reassured him, changing the subject. "Dr. Lewis is head of the department. I'm sure he's the one taking care of her."

"I'm not the one taking care of her, but I can tell you that it's started," Dr. Lewis said from the doorway to the waiting room. Trevin and Michelle looked over.

"I thought you were the only one who specialized in—" Michelle started.

"Demons and humans," Dr. Lewis stated. "Why would I want to treat witches?"

"Rubeus mentioned you weren't too happy about

that," Trevin said. Dr. Lewis looked over at him. "You're not as I remember."

"It's a disguise," Dr. Lewis replied as he pulled the charm out, showing Trevin. "Everyone in this realm knows me as Dr. Lewis."

"You know each other?" Michelle asked, finally moving away from the window.

"He practically raised me," Trevin started to explain. "This is —"

"Speak another word, and I'll rip your tongue out of your goddamn mouth," Rubeus said as he came back in with two coffees. He handed Michelle one. Michelle was surprised he got her anything at all.

"That's a little uncalled for, don't ya think?" Trevin asked.

"He hasn't told her," Dr. Lewis replied.

"Told me what?" Michelle asked.

"No, I haven't," Rubeus said, ignoring her question. "It'd be nice if she could actually find something out through me instead of you."

"If she had to wait on you to tell her something that involves you, she'd be waiting an eternity," Trevin retorted.

"No, she wouldn't," Rubeus said, anger rising.

"Go on and tell her then," Trevin challenged, stepping up to him.

"I wasn't planning on telling her today," Rubeus said with a sudden eerie calmness. The energy in the entire room changed, throwing everyone off. "Today is *your* day. I'm not getting accused of taking it away. Who knows when you'll have another one?"

"And there it is," Trevin said, eyes dilating as he started to go for him.

"Stop it! Both of you," Michelle yelled as she put Trevin in a bubble.

"Release me!" Trevin slammed his fists against it.

"Not until you get ahold of yourself," Michelle said. Rubeus sat down and stretched his legs out as he grabbed a magazine. "I don't think Alyssa would want you beat up today."

"It wouldn't be me getting beat up," Trevin promised as he beat against the bubble with swirls of black energy.

"You know that wouldn't be the case," Michelle replied. She pushed him down in a chair on the opposite side of the room with the bubble before letting go of her hold on it.

"Is it like that every day with those two?" Dr. Lewis asked.

"Seems like it," Michelle responded.

"Like you would know," Trevin said under his breath.

Rubeus looked over at him and narrowed his eyes. Someone else came into the room and called Dr. Lewis away.

"What?" Michelle asked.

Trevin opened his mouth to speak.

"You better chose your next words wisely," Rubeus threatened.

Trevin said nothing, crossed his arms and looked away.

Michelle looked over at Rubeus. "So, are you going to tell me?"

"Not today," Rubeus said, continuing to look through the magazine.

Michelle closed her eyes as she clenched her fists and took a deep breath. She grabbed her stuff and walked out.

"Keep pushing her away," Trevin said under his breath.

"What was that?" Rubeus asked, looking over at him.

"You heard me."

"Things can't get any worse between us," Rubeus said as he put the magazine down.

"She can divorce your ass," Trevin replied.

"She wouldn't," Rubeus said confidently.

***

Dr. Lewis saw Michelle exit the elevator on the first floor and quickly head for the exit. She looked upset.

"Leaving already?" Dr. Lewis asked as he caught her at the entrance. She stopped and wiped her eyes before turning to face him.

"Yes. I can't take another minute with those two," Michelle admitted. "Tell Alyssa I'm sorry." She started to turn to leave.

"Is there anything I can do?" Dr. Lewis asked, reaching out for her.

"Maybe if you told me what Rubeus is keeping from me," Michelle suggested. "Seeing as it involves you."

"I'm sorry, but if it's his wish to be the one to tell you, then I can't," Dr. Lewis responded.

"I can respect that," Michelle said as she glanced at the charm. "What do you need a disguise for?"

"It was for something that happened twenty-three years ago," Dr. Lewis said. "I guess I really don't need it anymore, but it would make things confusing for my patients."

"It was to keep you safe from Bane, wasn't it?" Michelle asked. "I know you're not a pureblood, but you must carry the gene for it."

"You're right," Dr. Lewis replied. "He killed my...."

"I'm sorry," Michelle said.

Dr. Lewis shrugged. "It was a long time ago."

"Can you take it off?" Michelle questioned. "I'd like to

see your true self."

"I'm afraid if I did that, it would give the secret away," Dr. Lewis responded.

"You're his father," Michelle stated.

"What brought you to that conclusion?" Dr. Lewis asked.

"Mainly Trevin saying you practically raised him," Michelle stated. "But you said it happened twenty-three years ago. That's how old Rubeus is. How long has he known?"

"A few days," Dr. Lewis answered.

"Why doesn't he want to tell me?" Michelle asked mainly herself as she looked away from him.

"Maybe it's his way of getting back at you for not telling him about Remus," Dr. Lewis stated. "You don't seem to be on good terms with each other."

Michelle gasped and covered her mouth. "I forgot all about that."

"If he's anything like me, he'll get over it quickly," Dr. Lewis said. "I can tell this fight is tearing him apart inside. It's taking everything he has to hold his ground with it, but he'll come around soon."

"Trevin isn't helping," Michelle replied.

"Trevin has a big mouth," Dr. Lewis said. "He always has." They were both silent for a moment. "Since you figured it out, there's no harm in showing you. Come with me." He led her to an empty room and took the charm off.

"Wow," Michelle said, looking him over. "So, do you come with another name too?"

"Ryan Timmons," Ryan replied. "It's a pleasure to officially make your acquaintance." He took her hand and kissed it softly. Michelle's heart skipped a beat, and she flushed a little. Her reaction and rise in essence, didn't go undetected. Ryan pulled her closer as her scent caused his eyes to dilate. "We could find other similarities if you'd like," he whispered in her ear as he felt her pulse quicken.

Michelle closed her eyes as he moved some hair from the side of her face. Her breath caught in her throat as his lips lightly brushed hers. She felt trapped in a trance as he tested to see how far she would let him go. Michelle finally gained some control and snapped a bubble around herself, cutting off the energy she wasn't meaning to emit as well as removing his hold on her. He shook his head as the lingering remains of lavender dissipated. His eyes returned to normal.

"As tempting as that is, I have to decline," Michelle responded.

"I apologize for that," Ryan said, slightly embarrassed. "But your essence is intoxicating."

"I'm sorry, I usually have more control over it," Michelle replied.

"You have a lot built up," Ryan stated.

"It's been a while," Michelle admitted. "I guess I'm easily —"

"It's my fault for provoking it," Ryan said, cutting her off. "I hope this won't ruin our relationship."

"It won't," Michelle replied. "I should get going." She disappeared.

***

Rubeus was on his way out when he saw Ryan step out of a room down the hall. He had the charm back on and was straightening his lab coat.

"On your way out?" Ryan asked as he approached him.

"Yeah, I'm not real fond of hospitals," Rubeus admitted. "Besides, all this fighting and arguing is taking its toll."

"Well, I'll make sure you're notified when she finishes the delivery," Ryan replied.

As he walked away, Rubeus caught the scent of lavender. "You run into Michelle?" Rubeus asked.

Ryan stopped and turned. "We talked briefly on her way out," Ryan confessed.

"Must have been a heated discussion," Rubeus said, a little suspicious.

"She was a bit emotional," Ryan responded. "You should tell her."

"I will the next time I see her," Rubeus said.

"Next time?" Ryan inquired.

"I'm not currently spending a lot of time at the manor," Rubeus informed him.

"Don't let this go too far," Ryan warned. "I'd hate to see it end because one or both of you are too stubborn to let whatever this is about go."

"Thank you for your concern, but we'll be fine."

CHAPTER 15

"I'm surprised Trevin isn't here," Michelle noticed as she looked around the room. She sat beside Alyssa and set a bag she had brought with her on the floor beside the chair she was in.

"He was. I told him to go home and sleep," Alyssa said, stretching and letting out a sigh. "I could use some of that as well."

"When are they going to release you?" Michelle asked.

"Some time today, I guess," Alyssa shrugged. "How are things with you? Getting any better?"

Michelle looked down at the floor. "I don't know," Michelle admitted. "I hardly see him."

"Where's he going?" Alyssa inquired.

"I'm pretty sure he's been staying at the mansion with Remus," Michelle replied, looking back up at Alyssa. "I never told him, so I'm sure he's pissed about that."

"You never told him about Remus?" Alyssa asked, surprised.

"I just forgot," Michelle said. "I thought he was dead for eight months. It wasn't exactly the first thing on my mind to share with him."

"What else is bothering you?" Alyssa asked.

"We're not here to talk about me," Michelle responded. "How are you and the baby?"

"We're fine," Alyssa said. "Spill it."

"What makes you think there's something else?" Michelle questioned.

"Because you're my best friend, and we grew up together," Alyssa said. "I know when something is bothering you." She moved the covers off her and scooted to the edge of the bed.

"I can't tell you because I'm not supposed to know either," Michelle stated.

"That's not the only thing," Alyssa continued to pry.

"To tell you the other thing, I would have to tell you the first," Michelle countered.

Alyssa rolled her eyes. "Stop making it complicated," Alyssa said. "I'm not going to say anything."

Michelle sighed. "Dr. Lewis's real name is Ryan Timmons."

"So what?" Alyssa said, unenthused.

"You do know what my name is now, right?" Michelle asked.

"It's Michelle Tim...oh." Alyssa's eyes lit up with surprise. "I thought he died."

"I guess they can both cheat death," Michelle muttered.

"So what's the other thing?" Alyssa asked. Michelle looked away. "No way!" Alyssa pushed Michelle.

"Keep your voice down," Michelle demanded in a soft voice. "And no. Something almost did, but I stopped it."

"I can't believe either one of you would," Alyssa whispered. "His own son's wife...." She shook her head in disbelief.

"It's been a while, so it doesn't really take much right

now," Michelle admitted. "I lost control for a split second, but that's all it took."

"You've gotta find some kind of release," Alyssa said. "Why don't you run?"

"I have," Michelle said. "It doesn't get rid of enough of it."

"You better lift the ban then," Alyssa recommended. "You're gonna get yourself in trouble."

"I don't want to be the one to give in." Michelle crossed her arms.

"Stop being stubborn."

"I'm not the one being stubborn," Michelle replied.

"You two were truly made for each other." Alyssa rolled her eyes. "Anyway, we need to go see that contact when I get out of here."

"You just had a baby," Michelle stated. "You don't need to go."

"It's Nerissa's contact—I have to be the one to set it up. Go work it out with Rubeus so we can do this. Remus will watch her."

Just then, Rubeus came in. "I know you just had a baby, but we need to start making progress with this," Rubeus said, not noticing Michelle.

"I'm fine, thanks, you insensitive prick," Alyssa said. Rubeus opened his mouth to respond but stopped. "We were actually just discussing that."

Rubeus looked over at Michelle. "You're not going."

"The hell I'm not," Michelle snapped as she stood.

"If you two are going to fight, go outside. I'm sick of it," Alyssa said before Rubeus could respond. "We're all going to go. I just need a few days once I'm released to set it up. Now please, both of you, just go."

"Fine. I need to talk to you anyway." Rubeus looked back at Michelle.

"Talk to this," Michelle said as she flipped him off before disappearing.

"You better do something about her, and quick," Alyssa said.

"I'm trying to," Rubeus admitted. He disappeared.

***

"Can't we just talk?" Rubeus asked as he found her in the manor. "I wanna tell you something."

"If it's about your dad, I already know," Michelle commented.

"Who told you?" Rubeus questioned. "It was Trevin, wasn't it?" He clenched his fists, starting to get angry.

"Nobody did. I figured it out for myself," Michelle stated. "When were you planning on sharing?"

"Right now, actually," Rubeus said, calmer.

"A week after finding out?" Michelle asked.

"You were keeping Remus being alive a secret," Rubeus responded. "When were you planning on sharing *that*?"

"I wasn't keeping it a secret," Michelle refuted. "I just forgot with, you know, finding out you weren't dead. It wasn't exactly at the top of my list of things to say to you, but you're too thick to realize that." Rubeus started to say something. "I'm done talking to you."

She walked out of the room, and he followed her. "Well, I'm not."

"Please just go," Michelle demanded, becoming angrier. "All we're doing is making it worse. Until we're both ready to resolve this, we should probably keep our distance."

"Then let me know when you're ready." He disappeared.

CHAPTER 16

It was a chillier afternoon than usual in the demonic realm as the four of them met outside the manor. Alyssa and Trevin were standing at the bottom of the steps to the wraparound porch. Rubeus was on the porch leaning over the railing, keeping his distance from everyone, while Michelle was sitting on the steps, staring off into the distance. The tension between them cut through the air like ice.

"So are we all ready?" Alyssa asked, looking at a map.

"What's the name of the place?" Rubeus inquired.

"Multiplicity," Alyssa answered.

"Where the hell's that?" Michelle asked with annoyance, directing her attention to the matter at hand.

"California," Alyssa stated, still engrossed in the map.

"How are we supposed to get there?" Trevin asked. "None of us have ever been there."

"One of us has," Alyssa said nonchalantly, looking at Michelle. The other two looked over at her.

Michelle folded her arms defensively. "I've never heard of that place."

"Well, from what I found, it's near the school you went to during your transfer semester our senior year," Alyssa explained. "It was just recently turned into a club. I think it used to be a multi-level theatre. Know where I'm talking about now?"

"You're the Apostle. You can go anywhere," Rubeus stated as he came down the steps.

"I don't know where that club is. I could get us in the general area, but Michelle could get us right in front of it," Alyssa replied. "Do you remember?"

"Yeah, I'm just trying to picture it."

"Well, this will be a pleasant ride," Rubeus said sarcastically while rolling his eyes and crossing his arms. Michelle shot off the steps.

"You can have the front seat then," Michelle retorted, grabbing his arm roughly. Trevin took Rubeus's other hand, and Alyssa took Trevin's just as Michelle closed her eyes. Energy sparked to life around her, then wrapped around everyone else. They blinked out in a flash of light and reappeared outside the club.

Michelle let Rubeus go and walked into the club. Excision's "Bring the Madness" blasted as the other three followed her in. It was an interspecies club that allowed admittance to all species 24/7. It was dark, with strobe lights and colored neon lights flashing everywhere.

"So where's this contact supposed to be?" Trevin asked loudly over the music.

"It's Nerissa's contact," Rubeus shrugged.

"I'll be right back," Alyssa called out. She vanished into the crowd of people dancing. The other three went to the bar off to the left. There were multiple levels to the club and several doors that took you to another area with a different style of music. Michelle ordered three shots as the boys ordered beer. The bartender set the beers down and poured the shots.

"No thanks." Trevin put his hand up.

"I'm not drinking like that tonight," Rubeus stated.

"Really?" Michelle asked with a slight attitude.

"We're here on business," Rubeus responded. "You shouldn't be drinking like that either."

Trevin put his fist to his mouth as they both watched Michelle take all three shots just to defy him. Rubeus narrowed his eyes at her. Michelle grabbed a drink off a tray that went by and left the bar to go to the dance floor.

"You're gonna be picking her up off the floor by the time we leave," Trevin said. "Is she still mad at you?"

"She barely speaks to me," Rubeus confessed.

"She'll see you now," Alyssa said as she came back. She looked around the bar. "Where's Michelle?"

"Out there somewhere." Rubeus nodded as he and Trevin got up. He gently grabbed Alyssa's arm and pulled her near so he wouldn't have to yell. "Keep an eye on her." She nodded at him in response.

The guys followed a woman in gypsy garb, who was waiting for them by the stairs, up to the next level and went into another room.

"As soon as I find her," Alyssa said to herself, scanning the crowd. She found Michelle out on the dance floor. "Great." She ordered a shot and took it before venturing into the unknown

***

"This way," the woman said as she turned to face forward, her long, tightly curled dark hair sweeping behind her. Rubeus and Trevin continued to follow the woman down a narrow hallway and into another room, where strings of beads in the doorway acted as a door. There was hardly any light. "Alyssa tells me you're interested in demon hunters."

She moved some furniture around so everyone could sit; her bracelets and necklaces clattered in the process.

"You could say that," Rubeus said, noticing her eerie midnight eyes for the first time. "What do you know?"

"Not too much. They are rare. There haven't been any around in a millennia," the woman said as she sat down. It was a tiny room and looked like people were brought back if they wanted their fortune told. "Please, have a seat." She gestured.

"No thanks, we don't plan on being here long," Rubeus stated, remaining on guard. "Just tell us what you do know."

"Alyssa mentioned you were impatient," the woman replied. "Most demon hunters send scouts out to find their prey before they actually make a move."

"How do we find their scouts?" Trevin asked.

"It's near impossible to find a scout. They can be in any form," the woman explained. "But my brother, Aiden, can. He has a very odd talent."

They heard movement in the back of the room and what sounded like someone struggling.

"What's that?" Rubeus inquired his attention now at the back of the room.

"Nothing you need to worry about," the woman said, getting up and blocking the doorway that led to there.

"Where can we find your brother?" Trevin asked.

"You don't," she said. "He'll find you."

"Let's go." Rubeus rolled his eyes. "I'm not finding this helpful." They started to leave.

"The trick is to find them before they latch themselves onto you. Once they do, you're as good as dead," the woman informed them. The guys left. "My scout is closer than you think. You won't be able to stop me." The woman's eyes flashed, and she changed forms. The shadows hid his true form as he pushed back a curtain. He opened a large chest, and the woman he was impersonating was inside, tied up and gagged. "And the best part is, he'll really be helping me and not even know it." The demon hunter laughed.

Rubeus and Trevin made their way back to the main area. "Push it (Instrumental Extended)" by Delorean was playing. Rubeus leaned over the railing, looking down at the dance floor, searching for Michelle.

"Well, that was cryptic." Trevin leaned over the railing beside his brother, joining him in the search. "What do you think?"

"I don't know," Rubeus admitted with slight defeat in his voice. "I guess we'll have to go with it. It's the only information we've got right now." Trevin looked over and studied his brother for a moment. Concern and worry were written all over him.

Rubeus finally spotted Michelle. She and Alyssa were dancing very closely with each other. Trevin followed his gaze.

"That's not like her," Trevin said. "Maybe we should —"

Rubeus grabbed his arm and stopped him from leaving. "Don't you wanna watch?"

"Yeah, but I was trying to be respectable," Trevin said as Rubeus let him go. They continued to watch them. Someone else in the corner of the club noticed them too.

Michelle glanced up and saw them watching. She whispered something to Alyssa, and they both laughed. They started to dance more inappropriately with each other and got close enough to make the guys think they're were going to kiss. Their arms were around each other when they looked up at them and smiled. They started to kiss as they disappeared. Rubeus noticed the man in the corner wink out almost simultaneously.

"Let's go," Rubeus said. They disappeared.

CHAPTER 17

Michelle and Alyssa didn't go back to the demonic realm. Instead, they stayed in the human realm, but back on the east coast. They reappeared on a trail on the side of one of the mountains that overlooked the city. They were laughing as they continued up the trail.

"The look on their faces was priceless," Michelle laughed. They stopped where they could continue going up to the right or walk several feet forward to get a great view of the city. They moved forward towards a rock wall built at the edge for safety. There were stone benches and two sets of coin-operated binoculars. A few feet from where they had come from, a makeshift shelter from the weather was carved into part of the mountain. The ceiling was made of stone and concrete, part of the foundation left of a castle that used to sit at the top of the mountain. The path stuck out a few feet farther than the ceiling.

"How long do you think we have before they find us?" Alyssa asked. She sat down on one of the stone slabs as Michelle looked out at the city. The sun was starting to rise.

"Probably not too long," Michelle replied. "I don't know how, but he can always find me." They heard something behind them. "See." Michelle turned around but didn't see anyone.

"You ladies are gonna attract the wrong kind of attention acting like that in public," a man said.

"Like from you?" Alyssa asked as she stood, preparing for a fight.

"No, I'm just here to make sure the other two won't hurt you."

"Aw, ya hear that? He's here to protect us," Michelle said sarcastically as she saw flashes of light farther down the path. "I hate to disappoint you, but we're not the ones that need it." The man turned around at hearing something and saw Rubeus and Trevin standing before him. He pulled out a cross and held it up in front of him.

"What is that supposed to do?" Rubeus asked as he grabbed the guy's wrist with the cross, causing him to drop it. Rubeus knocked some of the edge of the foundation off and grabbed the guy's other wrist. He lifted him up and placed his wrists in the chunk he'd ripped out. Trevin handed him some mud mixed with some of the debris from the foundation. Rubeus put the mix over his wrists and heated it until it hardened. They both stepped back as the man hung by his wrists.

"Why are you following them?" Trevin started the interrogation.

"I could ask you the same thing," the man replied as he tried to pull his wrists free. "I'm here to stop you from taking advantage of them."

Rubeus and Trevin busted out laughing. "How's that working out for you?" Rubeus asked.

"Let me down, and I'll show you," the man threatened as he tried to kick him.

"What's your name?" Trevin asked.

"Aiden?" Michelle asked, surprised, as she walked up beside Rubeus. A few rays of sun from the sunrise washed over Aiden's face, showing his short brown hair and blue eyes. It also caught part of Trevin's arm, singeing it. He moved into the protection of the mountain.

"Michelle? I thought that was you, but—" Aiden started.

"*You're* Aiden?" Rubeus asked with slight disgust.

"Yeah—" Aiden started as he turned back to Michelle.

"You know him?" Michelle asked Rubeus suspiciously.

"No, his sister mentioned him back at the club," Rubeus explained. "How do *you* know him?"

"He's my ex-boyfriend," Michelle answered a little too defensively.

"What?" Rubeus asked, looking at Alyssa for confirmation. She nodded in agreement. He looked back at Aiden, sizing him up. He had a rugged appearance and almost matched him in looks and physical fitness.

"Well, technically, we never broke up," Aiden stated. "You disappeared."

"And you apparently never looked for me," Michelle replied, crossing her arms.

"I wasn't in town yet when it happened," Aiden said defensively. "I went to see you after I arrived, but your aunt said you were abducted by demons. How was I supposed to look for you?"

"As much as I would *love* to watch you two reconnect, we have more important matters to deal with," Rubeus said with a hint of jealousy.

"And the sun is almost up," Trevin added.

"Let him down then," Michelle requested.

"There's no way that's happening now," Rubeus said,

crossing his arms.

"If he's to help us, you're gonna have to," Trevin responded.

"Help with what?" Aiden asked.

"Finding scouts," Trevin answered.

"I actually thought that's what you were," Aiden admitted.

"And you came so highly recommended," Rubeus remarked.

"They aren't easy to spot," Aiden informed him. "They can be anyone or anything. Any of you could be one, and the others would never know it. But there's always something off with them."

"So, can you help us or not?" Trevin asked.

"Not from this vantage point," Aiden snapped. "I'll need to go to your realm and scout the place out."

"So you can go back and tell the demon hunter the layout? I don't think so," Rubeus said.

"I'm not a scout," Aiden said, getting angry.

"Exactly what one would say," Rubeus said.

"This is ridiculous," Michelle rolled her eyes and got him down. "He isn't a scout."

Aiden shook his arms out and rubbed his wrists. Blisters had formed on them from the heat.

Michelle looked at Rubeus. "Do you mind?"

"You're joking," Rubeus said.

"No, I'm not," Michelle replied.

Rubeus scowled at her as he grabbed Aiden's wrists. Aiden watched in amazement as the blisters went away.

"You can obviously travel, so we'll see you on the other side," Rubeus stated.

"I don't travel," Aiden admitted. "I'm able to ride the

energy waves left behind when someone does."

"You can ride his waves then." Rubeus possessively pulled Michelle to him and disappeared with her.

"I don't think he likes me very much," Aiden said.

"What gave ya that idea?" Trevin asked. "I'll take you to my place to give them time to cool down after the fight they're gonna have." The three of them disappeared.

***

"Boyfriend?" Rubeus asked. Michelle rolled her eyes as she sat down on the couch. "You never mentioned him when you first arrived here."

"Would it have mattered?" Michelle countered. "Besides, we weren't together then."

"He seems to think so," Rubeus stated.

Michelle sighed with defeat. "Fine. The beginning part of my senior year, I went to California for a quarter of the year. I met him while I was there. When I came back here, he visited me once a month and eventually said he was going to quit his job and move out here to be with me. The last few months leading up to graduation, I didn't see or hear from him, so I assumed he had changed his mind or met someone else. Then I came here, and you know the rest." She moved to a window and looked out it.

"Do you still have feelings for him?"

"No, I was never in love with him," Michelle answered as she stared off into nothing. "I know we've been at each other a lot lately, but you don't need to worry about him."

"I'm not worried about that," Rubeus said. "It was just a surprise."

"You don't indulge in your past relationships either," Michelle added as she looked over at him.

"There's no need to with a brother like mine," Rubeus

stated.

Michelle smiled. "Well, for what it's worth, I don't believe half the stuff he tells me about you anyway."

"Only half? So much weight has been lifted," Rubeus joked. Michelle laughed. He came up behind her and wrapped his arms around her. She leaned up against him, missing his touch. "Maybe we should sit down and actually get to know each other better."

"It's not that we don't know each other. I mean, we spent over a year together beforehand," Michelle said. "We've just never gotten on a personal level with each other."

"I wasn't allowed to get personal during your training," Rubeus admitted. "So much has happened since then. We haven't really had time for anything else."

"I know," Michelle agreed. "It's one thing after the other lately."

"Yeah," he said. "It's getting late. I'm going to bed." He kissed her on the cheek before letting her go. "Should I expect you?"

"You're staying here tonight?" Michelle asked.

"Yeah, unless you don't want me to," Rubeus said.

"I'll be up in a few," Michelle said. He started up the stairs. "Hey." He stopped and looked over. "I love you."

"I love you too," They smiled at each other, and he continued his way up.

CHAPTER 18

"Sorry, I thought Trevin was in here," Rubeus said as he started to walk into Jade's room. It screamed girl, with pink walls and orchid carpet.

Alyssa turned and looked back at him. "It's fine," she said. "Actually, you can help me."

"That's all right." Rubeus put his hands up. "I can go find someone." He turned to leave.

"There's no time for that," Alyssa said. "I just need to get these sheets up and changed out before I lay her back down. She made a mess everywhere." Rubeus sighed and came back in. He started to grab the sheets in the crib. "No, you don't want to touch those. Here." She handed him Jade, instead. He had a hold of her under the arms and out away from him. "She doesn't have the plague." Rubeus didn't move. "Have you never held a baby?"

"I really don't—," he started as she put her in his arms properly.

"Keep her head supported," Alyssa said. "I'll be right back. I'm gonna put these in the wash."

"That wasn't part of the deal," Rubeus called after her. She waved her hand at him as she left the room.

He looked down at his niece with her already full head

of curly teal hair. She stared back up at him with big gray eyes, smiled at him, and giggled. Michelle peeked in after running into Alyssa in the hall downstairs.

"That's a nice look for you." Michelle leaned against the doorframe and crossed her arms.

Rubeus looked over at her. "Yeah, well, this wasn't my idea," Rubeus replied. Jade sneezed, and a huge snot bubble blew out of her nose. "Gross."

"Really?" Michelle laughed, fully walking into the room. "You pull people apart, and you think that's gross?" She grabbed a tissue and handed it to him. "Clean her up, and I'll think about taking her off your hands." He took the tissue and wiped her nose off. Michelle went to take Jade, but the baby grabbed ahold of Rubeus's shirt. "She doesn't want me to take her."

"Well, she doesn't get a say in it," Rubeus replied as he tried to hand her off. Jade started to cry.

"Sorry, you're stuck with her." Michelle smiled. Jade immediately stopped crying as Rubeus kept her. "She likes you."

"I have things I need to do," Rubeus said as he sat down in a rocking chair beside the crib. Michelle sat on the bed in the room to the left of the chair and crib. Jade curled into his arms and fell asleep. Michelle saw him soften at it and smiled at him. "You really want one of these?"

"Eventually, yes," Michelle stated. "But I know —"

"Look, I'm sorry for not telling you when I found out, and I swear to you I had nothing to do with it." Alyssa and Trevin heard them talking and stopped in the hallway, right before the door, and listened. "I'm not great at this kind of thing, but believe it or not, I was upset too."

"What about the other times?" Michelle asked.

"There were only two other times," Rubeus confessed. "I was barely a teenager and scared shitless. I went to Remus for help, and he gave me options. I chose to make a potion to force a miscarriage both times. And before you say anything, yes, I used protection. You're actually the first I've not used it with."

Alyssa and Trevin finally came back in. Alyssa put fresh sheets down.

"You got her to fall asleep?" Alyssa looked surprised. "It takes me hours most of the time. I'm afraid to take her from you."

Trevin came farther in and sat beside Michelle.

"She's taken a liking to him," Michelle said.

"I don't see how. He's so cold hearted," Trevin replied.

"You can add this to the list of things I'm better at than you," Rubeus shot back.

Trevin's face showed annoyance as he got up. "Give her to me," Trevin demanded. He gently took her from him and laid her in her crib. Jade started to stir as Trevin and Alyssa held their breath. She fell back asleep, and they let their breath out.

"Let's go," Alyssa whispered. The four of them quietly left the room, and Alyssa shut the door. "You know, it'd be nice if she had a playmate to grow up with."

"Then have another kid," Rubeus countered.

"One's enough for now," Trevin said. They went downstairs and outside.

"We'll wear you down eventually," Alyssa said.

Rubeus looked back at them and smiled as he shook his head.

"Let her fall asleep in his arms a few more times, and you'll have him," Michelle said to them softly before going down the steps to catch up to him. They linked hands and continued towards the manor.

"That can be arranged," Alyssa said, leaning against Trevin.

He put his arm around her. "He'll break sooner than you think."

Chapter 19

Michelle walked into the kitchen of the manor and sat a speaker down on one of the countertops. She linked her phone to it via Bluetooth and picked a rock playlist. She hit play and started pulling out cleaning supplies from the closet in the back corner. Michelle pulled her hair back with a bandana and started to clean. Breaking Benjamin's "Close to Heaven" came on in the middle of her progress, so she turned it up and softly sang to the parts she knew. Towards the end of it, Rubeus came up behind her and wrapped his arms around her.

"Sorry if I woke you." Michelle turned the music down a little.

"I needed to get up anyway," Rubeus said.

Michelle started putting things back on the island in the center of the room. A can of cooking spray fell over and rolled off the island, so Michelle bent over to pick it up. Rubeus looked her over as she did. As she put the spray back on the counter, he spun her around and pinned her to the island. Michelle saw the intent in his eyes as he hesitated for a brief moment. When she didn't stop him or protest, he kissed her, pushing everything off the island as he lifted her by her thighs and sat her on it.

"Look at the mess you just made," Michelle said, looking down at the floor, not believing he just did that.

Rubeus shrugged it off as he pulled her underwear down and off, leaving her skirt on. She wrapped her arms around his neck as he pushed into her. They kissed again, suppressing a moan that was escaping her lips.

Alyssa opened the front door and walked into the foyer, and continued down the hallway that went past the stairs.

"Hey, have you guys seen any extra bottles?" Alyssa called out from the other room, on her way to the kitchen since she heard the music. "I looked everywhere at our house, but—"

Without looking or pulling away from Michelle, Rubeus threw his arm out, and the door to the kitchen slammed shut before Alyssa made it to them. He turned his wrist, and it locked.

"Really?" Alyssa asked as she jiggled the doorknob. She tried to teleport in but couldn't. Michelle had put a shield around the inner walls of the kitchen, preventing anyone from getting in. Rubeus and Michelle laughed as they continued.

"Maybe we should finish somewhere else," Michelle suggested.

"This is our house; she shouldn't barge in like that," Rubeus replied.

"I don't know how long I can hold it," Michelle admitted as he went harder.

"Distracted?" Rubeus smiled.

Michelle pressed her lips to his as she gripped him tighter. The door unlocked and slightly opened as they disappeared.

***

Alyssa slowly pushed the door open and peeked in. "Hello?" she asked cautiously. She pushed the door all the way open and turned the music off as she looked around. There was stuff all over the floor.

Trevin appeared beside her and sat up on the island. "What's taking so long?" he asked as Alyssa noticed some clothing on the floor.

"I don't think I'd sit there if I were you," Alyssa replied. Trevin looked down at the floor and quickly got off the island. "I think I interrupted."

They looked out the doorway to the kitchen when they heard voices in the other room. Alyssa and Trevin stepped out of the kitchen and into the open area by the front entrance to the manor.

"That's today?" Michelle asked as she and Rubeus stopped by the door.

"You can be late," Rubeus responded. "I'll see you in a bit." He kissed her deeper than she was expecting before walking out the door. Michelle turned with a smile on her face when she saw Alyssa and Trevin.

"Hey," Michelle said, stunned, like a teenager who had just been caught by her parents. Alyssa and Trevin were just staring at her with their arms crossed.

"What's with him?" Alyssa inquired. "He's been awfully cheery and nice lately."

Michelle shrugged her shoulders as she walked by them and back into the kitchen. "I think he's trying to make up for everything," Michelle said. "Plus, Aiden hasn't been around."

"I've been keeping him away with meaningless tasks." Alyssa leaned on the counter.

"This place looks like a tornado hit it," Trevin stated.

"It's not that bad. I just cleaned in here." Michelle wiped the center island down again.

"Sure," Alyssa said, sliding her clothes to her with her foot. Michelle glanced down and picked it up. "I take it you're not withholding anymore."

"We were finally able to talk it out without getting angry at each other," Michelle said as she started picking everything off the floor. "You're looking for bottles?" she asked, changing the subject. "There are some in the dishwasher."

Alyssa opened the dishwasher and grabbed the bottles. "Thanks," she said. "So, what's going on tonight?"

"Aiden is supposed to be going before all the elders to explain how he's going to find the demon hunter," Michelle replied.

"Oh, I should be there."

"No, you don't," Michelle stated. "This is our realm. Let us handle it."

"It's my responsibility, too," Alyssa argued.

"On a much larger scale," Michelle added. "You don't need to micromanage. I'll see you later." She disappeared, and Alyssa sighed.

"Don't get so upset over it," Trevin said as he put his arm around her. "This realm has survived millennia with an Apostle that really didn't care what happened to it."

"I'd like to do a better job than him," Alyssa fretted.

"You're gonna have to go through Rubeus for more involvement," Trevin said. "This is his realm now. Let him do his job. If they can't handle it, then you step in."

CHAPTER 20

Michelle appeared outside of City Hall and walked up the steps. Susan looked up from her desk as she opened the doors. She started to say something as Michelle made her approach, but Michelle held her hand up, already knowing what she was going to say. She walked past her without a word and into the elevators.

"Nice of you to show up," Camilla commented as Michelle came into the room.

"Rubeus knew I was running behind," Michelle replied, taking her seat at the table.

"She shouldn't get special treatment because she's your wife," Camilla stated, clearly upset about it.

"She's not," Rubeus responded sternly. Camilla harrumphed. "Is there a problem?"

"You've both been neglecting your duties," Camilla rebutted. "Neither of you have hardly been here in weeks. You're letting your personal lives get in the way, which is why demons shouldn't marry, let alone both have a seat on the council."

Sven and Arixanna came in with Aiden. The others didn't notice.

"We haven't been neglecting anything," Michelle

stated. "The majority of those past few weeks were spent waiting to hear back from Nerissa."

"That's something else we need to discuss," Camilla stated. "The two of you haven't been around long enough—"

"I can assure you we know how dangerous she is," Rubeus said with an annoyed tone.

"Then why are you putting our fate in her hands?" Camilla demanded.

"We're not," Michelle snapped. "We have nothing else to go on. There isn't information on demon hunters anywhere. She's the only one who knows something."

"My brother knew about them," Camilla muttered.

"Your brother sealed his fate when he turned against his own kind," Rubeus stated harshly.

"He didn't turn against anyone."

"Just purebloods," Rubeus countered.

Camilla fell silent until trying another angle. She was clearly in a mood to fight. "You're letting someone we don't know into our realm."

"I know him," Michelle said.

"I understand your concern, but you can trust me," Aiden informed them. The three looked over, finally aware of his presence.

"I'll be the judge of that," Camilla responded.

"Have a seat," Sven suggested.

Aiden sat down in a chair that faced a rectangular table. Sven and Arixanna joined the other three at the table.

"You're both on the council?" Aiden asked, looking at Michelle and Rubeus. "Great."

"So, how are you going to find these scouts?" Rubeus questioned.

"I don't really know how to explain it, but—" Aiden

started.

"We're supposed to rely on something you can't even explain?" Camilla rudely interrupted. "You might as well go ahead and condemn us all to death."

Rubeus glared over at Camilla.

"I can show you," Aiden stated. "With your permission, of course."

Rubeus nodded at him. Aiden stood up and closed his eyes. An eerie green light softly emitted from him until it surrounded his silhouette.

"What is he doing?" Arixanna asked, the others startled too. As he opened his now glowing green eyes, Michelle formed a shield between the elders and Aiden.

"Relax, it doesn't hurt you," Aiden said as he returned to normal. He had seen what he wanted to.

"What was that?" Michelle asked, lowering the shield.

"I call it my second sight. It enables me to see energy signatures and auras," Aiden explained. "Each species leaves a specific pattern. Your kind used me the first time they appeared. It's the only reason you're still here."

"We're still here because the demon hunters started going after the witches too," Sven stated. "It took both species to beat them back."

"Their goal was to get rid of the purebloods, which they succeeded in doing," Camilla added.

"That may be, but I was still there," Aiden said.

"What are you?" Arixanna asked, obviously intrigued.

"I'm human, but with talents," Aiden answered.

"Then how could you survive all this time?" Camilla asked.

"I was reincarnated throughout the millennia," Aiden clarified. "The memories of my predecessors were passed down each time in case I would be needed again."

"We'll have to cross reference that information," Sven replied.

"You won't find anything," Aiden said. "If nothing was written about demon hunters, I wouldn't be mentioned either."

"So what do you need from us in order to find them?" Rubeus asked.

"Just time," Aiden said. "And the freedom to move about as I please. I need to reacquaint myself to the area in order to determine what's different."

"You expect us to just let you roam around?" Camilla distrusted.

"Your request is granted—" Rubeus started.

"What?" Camilla asked disapprovingly. "We need to discuss this first."

"You didn't let me finish," Rubeus snapped.

Camilla stood. "I can't sit back and keep quiet anymore."

"Then leave," Rubeus suggested. "And wait for me outside."

"Gladly," Camilla said as she started to leave.

"But know if you lose, which you will, you're relinquishing your position," Rubeus informed her. Sven and Arixanna gasped as Camilla gave him a shocked look.

"Are you serious?" Michelle whispered. He held his hand up to silence her as he and Camilla kept their eye contact. Michelle and Aiden were the only ones that didn't know what was really going on.

"That's a little premature," Camilla said, trying to keep her poise. "Your arrogance and overconfidence are going to be your downfall."

"We can do this now, or after we're finished here," Rubeus stated. "I don't care either way." Camilla considered her options, knowing he was right that she didn't stand a chance if she went through with her challenge. Rubeus sensed her remission. "I suggest you sit down and shut up." Camilla sat down with a defeated look on her face. "As I was saying. You're free to move about as you please, but only under constant supervision. The five of us will rotate out with you. Camilla, you'll have the first rotation."

"What? She'll kill me," Aiden protested.

"She won't lay a hand on you," Rubeus promised. "Isn't that right?" He looked over at her.

"I won't harm him," Camilla said softly, not looking up.

"You're free to go," Rubeus said.

Everyone got up. Rubeus stepped out as Camilla took Aiden out of the room.

"What was that?" Michelle inquired.

"She challenged his position," Sven said.

"I don't know what made her think she would be successful," Arixanna stated. "But it now puts you in her position."

"I don't understand," Michelle replied.

"If you challenge and lose, you completely give up your seat of power, but if you retract it, you lose your rank among the rest of the elders. She's now at the bottom," Arixanna explained. "Remus was below her, so now you move up, followed by Sven, me, and now Camilla."

"That doesn't seem fair."

"She knew the consequences when she did it," Rubeus said as he came back in.

"I'm surprised you stayed as calm as you did," Sven

said.

"Camilla is the least of my worries," Rubeus responded.

"Do you really trust her not to harm him?" Arixanna asked.

"She's finished if she does," Rubeus stated. "She knows that."

He went to the table and started to gather up the paperwork. Michelle and Sven continued talking as Arixanna approached Rubeus. She sat on the table next to where he was standing.

"How long are these rotations going to be?" Arixanna inquired.

"I'm not sure yet," Rubeus confessed. "We need to divide the realm up into sections for each of us to cover."

"Well, I'll take the next one," she said as she leaned back on her hands.

He glanced over at her. "Don't tell me you're actually interested in that," Rubeus responded. "He's a human, so he claims."

"I'm just intrigued," Arixanna admitted. "A human with a special power. You don't come across that very often."

"Well, he's also Michelle's ex-boyfriend," Rubeus stated.

"And you're mine. We can call it an even trade then," Arixanna replied.

"That's hardly an even trade," Rubeus said. "I don't know if she'd go for that."

"Why do you care?" Arixanna asked. "Jealous?"

"Jealous? No. A little concerned for your wellbeing? Yes," Rubeus half joked.

"I knew you still cared about me." Arixanna smiled.

"Well, yeah. I'll always care about you," Rubeus said.

They were both silent for a few minutes.

"Do you ever regret it?" Arixanna finally asked.

"That's something I've tried not to think about," Rubeus said. "We both made the right choice for the situation at the time."

He turned and put his back against the table, crossing his arms. They both watched Sven and Michelle. Michelle glanced over and smiled at him before turning back to Sven.

"It worked out great for you," Arixanna said as she got off the table. Rubeus started to say something. "Don't even say it. I have high expectations that no one can fill because of you." She left the room.

CHAPTER 21

Rubeus was sitting at the dining room table, propping his head up with his fist. He picked at his food until he finally pushed it away.

"What's wrong?" Michelle asked as she walked back in. "You've been depressed ever since City Hall."

"I'm not depressed," Rubeus said. "Just thinking."

"About what she said?" Michelle questioned as she took his plate.

"What who said?" Rubeus asked.

"Arixanna," Michelle answered from the kitchen.

"You heard all that?"

"We were in the same room," Michelle said, stating the obvious. "And I am a pureblood."

He went to the kitchen doorway and leaned against it, hands in pockets. "I was planning on telling you about her."

"I already knew," Michelle responded.

"Nothing gets past you," Rubeus stated. "How'd you figure this one out? Wait, let me guess. Trevin."

"No. It's the way you two are around each other," Michelle said. "The way she looks at you when you're not paying attention. She still loves you."

"No, she doesn't." Rubeus shook his head. "It was

seven years ago."

"She still feels something for you," Michelle insisted. "Maybe not as strong, but it's still there."

"Either way, you don't need to worry about her," Rubeus assured her.

"I'm not," Michelle said. "You are right about one thing, though...," she started as she walked towards him.

"What's that?" He asked.

"It's *far* from an even trade." Michelle brushed against him on her way out.

"You said you didn't...." Rubeus thought out loud, following her into the other room.

"I know, but I didn't say we didn't do other things." Michelle smiled. She went to look back at him, but he was right there on her, startling her. His eyes were beginning to dilate as he pinned her against the back of the couch.

"Like what?" he inquired.

She wrapped her arms around him and smiled. "I'll show you."

She disappeared with him as they started to kiss.

CHAPTER 22

Aiden was outside on the porch at Trevin and Alyssa's house. Camilla had dropped him off not too long ago. He leaned over the railing, looking out towards the manor. It was a distance away, but close enough to barely make out movement if someone was outside.

"Give it up," Trevin said as he stepped outside with Jade, holding a bottle. "He won't let you get close to her."

"I'll get my chance to talk to her when it's her turn," Aiden said confidently. "Why is he so protective of her anyway?"

"Really?" Trevin asked, slightly surprised. "I thought it was obvious. They're married."

Aiden looked back at him, shocked. "What? I didn't think demons married."

"We don't," Trevin confirmed as he sat down in a rocking chair.

"It's just as well," Aiden replied with a sigh. "She became a lost cause the day she was abducted."

"Well, I don't want to give you false hope because nothing can split those two up, but interspecies relationships aren't unheard of," Trevin said. "Look at me."

"Yeah, you're with a witch, right?" Aiden questioned.

He turned and put his back to the railing.

"Technically, yes, but she's now part demon since she became the Apostle."

"May I?" Aiden asked, wanting to hold Jade.

Trevin looked around for Alyssa first. "Sure," he said as he handed her off.

"What is she going to be?" Aiden inquired.

Trevin handed him the bottle, and Jade immediately grabbed for it. Aiden smiled slightly.

"We think she'll have both, but we won't know for sure until she starts exhibiting her power," Trevin said. "What about you?"

"What do you mean?" Aiden looked over at Trevin.

"Are you really human?" Trevin leaned forward, resting his elbows on his knees. "Humans aren't supposed to have any kind of power."

"I've never been told otherwise." Aiden thought for a minute. "Humans have abilities too, just not usually in the form of energy like you." Jade finished the bottle, and he handed her back to Trevin. "What's your brother's deal? Sunlight doesn't hurt him?"

"He's a pureblood," Trevin stated.

"What does that mean?" Aiden asked. "Camilla mentioned them earlier."

"How do you not know?" Trevin gave him a quizzical look.

"There aren't a lot of demons in California."

"Basically, the rules you know about demons don't apply to him," Trevin started to explain. "Purebloods were the first created by the witches. They're supposed to be the perfect species."

"So he can be out during the day, take whoever he

wants without permission, and doesn't have to leave because he was told to?" Aiden asked. Trevin nodded. "You know how dangerous that makes him?"

"Yeah," Trevin said matter-of-factly.

"I thought they were all killed in the war," Aiden said.

"They were, but as the witch elders started to die off, so did the spells they cast over us," Trevin continued. "Rubeus and Michelle are the first two to be born since then."

"Spells cast?" Aiden questioned.

"You're better off learning our history in the texts written about it," Trevin said. "Besides, you don't need to know it."

"So Michelle is one too," Aiden thought out loud. "They're going to be the demon hunter's primary targets."

"I know," Trevin said with concern. "That's why Rubeus wants to stop them. I don't think he cares what happens to him. He just wants Michelle to be safe."

"He's willing to sacrifice himself for her?" Aiden asked. "That's un-demon like."

"We're not all savage beasts. Most of us are quite civilized," Trevin said, a little offended. "Besides, he'll do anything for her. Even if it means dying."

Aiden got chills as he looked back over towards the manor.

CHAPTER 23

Michelle was in the bathroom putting on the finishing touches while Rubeus waited for her in the bedroom. He was stretched out on the bed with his back against the headboard and his arms up behind his head.

"Don't you think it'll be kinda awkward?" Michelle called from the bathroom.

Rubeus had just started to doze off and cracked an eye open. "Why would it be awkward?" he asked. "You know everyone that'll be there."

"I don't know," Michelle said lightly.

The whole family, minus Camilla since she was out with Aiden, was having dinner together at the mansion in the human realm. Michelle never had family get-togethers growing up, considering all she knew from her family at the time was her aunt, and they didn't get along. Rubeus stepped up to the doorway as Michelle put a hand on her stomach.

"You all right?" Rubeus had a concerned look on his face.

"Yeah, I guess it's just nerves," Michelle said. She took one last look at herself in the mirror.

"You look beautiful," Rubeus stated. "You always do."

She smiled at him through the mirror. "I guess I'm

ready."

Rubeus offered his hand. Michelle took it, and he brought her near as they disappeared.

Trevin and Alyssa were already there when Michelle and Rubeus arrived at the mansion. They had gotten there early so they would have plenty of time to put Jade down for her nap.

"What's with all the decorations outside?" Rubeus asked. "We've never celebrated the holidays."

Remus shrugged. "It seemed fitting. And I didn't want to look like an outcast, being the only house with nothing up. Everyone already steers clear of this part of town."

"I don't see that as a bad thing," Trevin commented. He handed Rubeus a drink and offered Michelle one. She put her hand up, declining. "I hear they call it the demon house now."

"It *is* full of demons," Michelle replied as she stepped into the kitchen. "What are you cooking?"

"I hope there's a backup plan if Remus is cooking," Ryan joked as he and Sven came in.

"I wasn't that bad of a cook," Remus countered.

"Sure you weren't." Rubeus rolled his eyes.

"You never complained," Remus responded in defense. "Why do you think I spent so much time in the human realm?"

"*I'm* cooking," Alyssa said. She joined Michelle in the kitchen. "With hopefully some help from you."

"Looks like you're doing fine." Michelle cracked open the oven. "I'd say another hour, and it'll be done." She put her hand on her stomach again as she closed the oven door.

"Are you okay?" Alyssa asked with concern, putting her hand on her arm.

"Yeah, I just haven't been feeling well lately," Michelle admitted.

Alyssa looked over at everyone else. They were all sitting in the living room talking. "You don't think...?" Alyssa asked softly.

"It crossed my mind," Michelle whispered. "I actually brought a test with me."

Alyssa squealed with excitement. A few of the guys looked over.

"We'll be right back," Alyssa called as she grabbed Michelle's arm and took off out of the room. A few minutes later, they were both sitting in the hallway outside one of the bathrooms, waiting. "So what are you gonna do if you are?"

"I don't know," Michelle stated, inspecting her fingernails. "I'm not sure how I would even tell him."

"Do you think he'd be happy?" Alyssa asked.

Michelle shrugged as she brought her knees up to her chest and wrapped her arms around them. They sat in silence until the timer Alyssa had set on her phone went off.

"I can't look," Michelle confessed. Alyssa got up and went into the bathroom. "Well?" she asked when Alyssa said nothing.

"Congratulations," Alyssa answered as she handed her the test.

Michelle looked down at it as panic washed over her. "I...I can't tell him," Michelle said in a nervous fluster.

"What? He needs to know," Alyssa said.

"I just can't," Michelle said, nearing tears. "Promise me you won't say anything. Not to Trevin. No one."

"Okay, I promise," Alyssa said. "But he's gonna find out eventually. You can't hide it."

"I'll find a way," Michelle said confidently. "We

should get back before they start to wonder." She stood up, took a deep breath, and slowly let it out to steady her nerves. "Okay." They both went back and joined the others.

Michelle started gathering dishes and taking them to the sink as everyone finished eating. Everyone moved back to the living room.

"You don't need to do that, you know," Remus said as he came in and pulled a pie from the fridge.

"I know," Michelle replied.

He could tell something was bothering her. "You know you can come to me about anything. We haven't talked in a while."

"I know, but I'm fine," Michelle lied as she started to load the dishwasher.

"I'm here if you need me," Remus said and went back to the living room.

Michelle stopped what she was doing and just watched everyone talking and laughing. She felt tears starting to form and looked away, putting her back to everyone. She looked up and saw Ryan standing before her, causing her to jump.

"You startled me," Michelle said as she turned back to the sink.

"You look unhappy," Ryan commented as he put some more plates in the sink.

"Just watching everyone getting along and actually caring about each other, forgetting about the problems at hand—I've never had that," Michelle replied. "My family's crazy."

"I doubt they were crazy."

Michelle looked over at him. "My mother wanted to kill me, my grandfather tried to kill me, and my aunt did kill me," Michelle informed him. "Doesn't get any more psychotic than that."

"Well, when you put that way," Ryan said, trying to make her smile.

"It just makes me wonder who I'm gonna try to kill," Michelle replied.

"You killed Bane, didn't you?" Ryan asked. "So you don't have to worry about it."

Michelle laughed a little. "I guess you're right. Thanks." She turned to him and wrapped her arms around him. He embraced her back.

"Besides, you have all of us now," Ryan said.

Rubeus looked over and gave him an odd look. Ryan motioned for him to come out.

"Everything all right?" Rubeus asked as he sat on a stool on the other side of the kitchen sink.

"She's fine," Ryan assured him as they let go. "Just a little homesick."

"Sorry." Michelle wiped tears from her eyes.

"You wanna go?" Rubeus asked.

"No, I'm all right," Michelle replied.

"Well, I'll let you take it from here," Ryan said.

He went back and joined the others. Alyssa looked over at them as they talked. Michelle leaned over the counter and kissed Rubeus.

CHAPTER 24

After a month of searching and a few mishaps, Michelle finally found a spell that concealed her pregnancy and symptoms. She laced a necklace she already had with the spell and put it on. The constant fatigue and nausea went away instantly, letting her know it was working.

She tucked the necklace under her shirt before coming up from the alchemy lab. Rubeus had gone for a late-night run and hadn't come back yet. Michelle grabbed a couple of bottles of water and went outside to wait for his return. She was leaning over the banister that wrapped around the entire manor when she saw a flash of light. Arixanna had returned with Aiden—Camilla's rotation had ended a few days ago. It had finally been decided that everyone would have a month since it would take a while to cover the entire realm. Once Arixanna finally left, she saw him start her way.

"It's been hell trying to talk to you," Aiden said, approaching the steps.

Michelle looked down at him. "How so?" Michelle asked, pretending to show interest.

"Rubeus doesn't want me around you."

"That's news to me," Michelle stated as she opened one of the bottles of water. "If he wanted to keep us apart, I wouldn't be part of the rotation. Besides, he isn't concerned with you."

"Is he around?" Aiden asked, scanning the area.

"I'm sure he's close by," Michelle said, taking a sip of water. "What did you want to talk about?"

"I know it doesn't matter anymore, but I wanted to explain why I lost touch with you." Aiden came up the front steps and leaned over the banister beside her.

"You're right. It doesn't matter," Michelle stated. "Even if we had kept in touch and you moved to be with me, it wouldn't have made a difference. I still would have been brought here. I'd still be where I'm at right now."

"This life has really changed you," Aiden commented.

Michelle shrugged as she drank more water. "If you'd seen the things I've seen and done the things I've done, it would change you too. So, what's with this second sight of yours?" It was Aiden's turn to shrug. "Is it always creepy looking?"

"No, that was mainly for show," Aiden admitted.

"Were you ever gonna tell me?" Michelle asked. "If things would have been different?"

"I don't know," Aiden replied. "You never mentioned you were a demon."

"I didn't know what I was, but I bet you did," Michelle came back. "I'm sure you used that sight on me."

"I use it on everyone, but there was always some kind of interference with you," Aiden confessed. "I knew you weren't human, but I couldn't tell if you were a demon or witch."

"Probably the locket I always had on," Michelle replied. "It suppressed the energy."

"Possibly."

"What do you see now?" Michelle asked, looking over at him.

He turned to face her and took her free hand. Aiden opened his sight to her, allowing her to see what he saw. Everything briefly disappeared, and there was nothing but darkness. The outline of everything around them shimmered into existence. Michelle saw streams of energy form all around them. She looked at herself and saw a beautiful deep blue wrapped with gold surrounding her. There was a third color, but very faint. He let go of her hand, and reality snapped back in an instant.

"You have the energy signature of a demon, but there's also something different," Aiden explained. "All demons have blue energy fields, but you and Rubeus have the gold."

"That must be what marks us as purebloods," Michelle said.

Aiden nodded. "There's still something different with yours. When I used it at City Hall, I could see a third color attached to yours, but now it's suppressed."

"What was it?" Michelle asked.

"It was purple," Aiden answered. "It radiated from inside the blue. It was beautiful, but I don't know what changed."

Michelle's thoughts went to the necklace she had on. "Who knows?" Michelle shrugged. "Maybe it's because you showed me."

"Maybe, but I doubt it," Aiden said, sensing she was keeping something from him.

Michelle looked out from the manor and saw Rubeus coming back. Aiden followed her gaze. "I should probably go."

"Don't leave on my account," Rubeus responded as he

came up the steps. Michelle handed him a water. He gave her a kiss before going inside.

"That's guy code for get out," Aiden whispered to her. She rolled her eyes. "I'll see ya later."

Michelle watched him disappear towards Trevin's house before going inside. Rubeus was already in the shower when she went upstairs. She sat down on the bed and waited for him to finish. A few minutes later, he stepped out.

"Sorry," Michelle said.

"For what?" he asked.

"You probably didn't want to come home to that."

"It really doesn't bother me," Rubeus said as he put a pair of sweats on. "You look better."

"I feel better," Michelle admitted.

"Good, I was starting to get a little worried."

"Why?" Michelle asked a little too quickly, her heart skipping a beat.

"I didn't know if it was going to turn into something serious," Rubeus said.

"You could just heal me," Michelle stated.

"I can heal injuries. Not illnesses."

"Well, that's nice to know," Michelle commented. They were both silent for a moment. Rubeus started to say something, but Michelle cut him off. "He wanted to tell me why he blinked out all those years ago, but I told him I really didn't care."

"Okay." Rubeus shrugged. "I wasn't gonna ask."

"You can't tell me you weren't curious," Michelle said.

"I'm more curious about what he showed you," Rubeus replied, crossing his arms, leaning up against the dresser.

A few water droplets glistened off his arms, drawing Michelle's attention. Her thoughts wandered for a brief second before she snapped them back.

"He showed me his second sight," Michelle said, looking back at his face. "It was amazing. Everything went dark and then sort of appeared again, but only the outlines of things. Energy trails were all over the place. He said demons are blue, but only you and I have gold wrapped around it."

"What was his?" Rubeus asked.

"I didn't really get a look at his," Michelle admitted.

Rubeus narrowed his eyes, but not at her. "I'm having trouble believing he's human," Rubeus stated. "And you had no idea about what he can do?"

"Not a clue," Michelle said. "Do you want me to try and find out more?"

"No," Rubeus said. "I'm gonna let Arixanna handle that. She wants to get to know him on a more personal level anyway."

"He'd probably be more inclined to tell *me*."

"That may be, but I think it's better if you don't have much contact with him," Rubeus said.

"You just said you didn't care," Michelle said, a little too defensively.

"I don't," Rubeus said sternly. "Just trust me on this."

"Okay," Michelle said, knowing he wasn't telling her something. "I will."

Chapter 25

Alyssa was sitting at the counter in the kitchen watching Michelle cut vegetables for dinner. Michelle took the celery and slid it from the cutting board into the pot. The pot had butter, garlic, and onion already in it, sizzling away.

"I love the smell of onions cooking." Alyssa closed her eyes and breathed in the smell of everything cooking. Michelle grabbed some carrots.

"Me too," Michelle smiled. She began to cut the carrots.

"I don't understand why you never went to cooking school," Alyssa said. Michelle looked back at her and their surroundings. Alyssa caught on. "Right."

"Well, I guess you could say I went to college," Michelle said.

"Yeah, you majored in demonology and got an 'A' because you slept with your teacher," Alyssa commented.

"Hey, I didn't sleep with him until afterwards," Michelle retorted, pointing the knife at her. They both laughed. Michelle moved some of the carrots into the pot before grabbing a few more.

"So why are we doing another dinner?"

"No one knows how much time Remus has left, so they all decided to get together at least once a month," Michelle explained. "They're coming here this time, obviously, since we went over there last time."

"You're gonna have more than just soup, right?" Alyssa inquired.

"Of course," Michelle stated.

"What's the main course?" Alyssa asked.

"I don't know. I thought about grabbing a human later," Michelle joked.

Alyssa gasped. "You eat humans?" Alyssa asked, shocked.

"Oh yeah, they're a delicacy," Michelle said, trying not to laugh.

Alyssa grabbed a hand towel and threw it at her. "You almost had me." Alyssa rolled her eyes.

"Will you stir that for me?" Michelle asked.

Alyssa got up and went to the pot. "With what?" Alyssa looked around.

"It's right there beside it," Michelle said, setting the knife down. As she turned, her finger slid against the blade. "Ouch!" She turned back and looked at her finger.

"Are you okay?" Alyssa asked. "Ew, you're gonna need stitches."

"No, I won't," Michelle said, preparing to brace herself for it. She breathed in as it hit her. She cried out as she fell to her knees.

"What's wrong?" Alyssa asked, starting to panic. She knelt in front of her.

"It hurts so bad," Michelle barely squeaked out.

Alyssa grabbed her wrist and saw every layer of skin and muscle close before her eyes. There was no scar or anything indicating she had been cut. Michelle leaned against the cabinets and steadied her breathing.

"You really do take on his ability." Alyssa stood in disbelief.

"I don't know how he endures it," Michelle said. "Healing is worse than the injury."

"He's had his whole life to master it," Ryan said from the doorway. Michelle and Alyssa looked over. "Is there something you'd like to share?"

Michelle looked away.

"Rubeus doesn't know," Alyssa finally answered as she pulled Michelle up.

"I'd like to keep it that way for now," Michelle added.

"How far are you?" Ryan asked, coming further into the kitchen.

"I don't know, two and a half months, maybe," Michelle guessed. Ryan looked her over. Michelle pulled the necklace out. "This suppresses the symptoms and keeps me from showing."

"Have you seen anyone?" Ryan questioned. Michelle shook her head. "Well, why didn't you come to me?"

"Because I didn't want you to have the burden of knowing and not saying anything to him," Michelle said. "Besides, it's just weird now, you being his father and all."

Ryan rolled his eyes. "That's ridiculous. You're coming with me for a checkup." He grabbed her wrist. "We won't be gone long," he said to Alyssa as he disappeared with her.

***

"Everything looks good," Ryan said as he knocked on the door and cracked it open.

"You can come in," Michelle responded as she finished getting dressed. "Thank you for not asking why I don't want to tell him or lecturing me on it."

"Your reasons for withholding is your business,"

Ryan stated. "You don't have to worry about me telling him. You've already stated you don't want him to know, so I'm legally bound."

"I'm going to tell him, I'm just afraid of how he'll react," Michelle confessed. "He's already worried about my safety with everything going on. I don't need to add this to it."

Ryan picked up her necklace from the counter. "You make this yourself?" Ryan inquired.

Michelle nodded as he put it on her. Her pregnant belly instantly disappeared, along with her fatigue.

"It's amazing work." He put his hand on her abdomen, half expecting it to stop where it had been.

"Whatever it takes, for now," Michelle replied.

"He's going to be furious, you know that," Ryan said.

"I know, but one thing I've learned is how to handle Rubeus when he's angry," Michelle said. "I'll tell him before it's—"

"He," Ryan interrupted. "It's a boy, and you're three and half months along, not two."

"Wonderful," Michelle replied, not enthused. "I need to get back and finish dinner."

"Of course," Ryan said. He took her hand and disappeared with her.

***

This time around, Michelle was more social and didn't object to someone else cleaning up after dinner. It wasn't long after when everyone, except Alyssa and Trevin, left. Alyssa had gone to put Jade down in the other room as Michelle went to the kitchen to see if anything else needed to be done. There were still a few plates and silverware from dessert that didn't fit in the running dishwasher left in the sink. She heard Trevin asking Rubeus some questions about how the search for the demon hunter was going as she knelt to pull the dish rack out from under the sink. Michelle laid a hand towel on the counter beside the sink and then put the dish rack over it. She filled one of the sink compartments with hot soapy water and the other with lukewarm water. Alyssa came into the kitchen as Michelle started washing what was left.

"That was quick," Michelle said, placing a plate in the lukewarm water. Alyssa pulled it out and placed it on the dish rack.

"It's getting easier to put her down," Alyssa said. "Especially since she's finally used to her schedule."

Michelle put the last plate and silverware in the other compartment. She felt around the soapy water for anything else as Alyssa took the dishes out of the water. Her eyes widened. "Oh no," Michelle whispered.

"What is it?" Alyssa asked.

Michelle glanced over at her as she pulled her hand out of the water. There was a tiny cut on it from a knife that was used to cut the cake. Someone must have put the plates over it, hiding it from view when she had filled the sink with water. "Oh." Michelle closed her eyes and tried to stifle a cry of pain as the healing sensation started. The guys looked over. Alyssa saw them and cried out louder than Michelle.

"What are you doing?" Michelle whispered.

"Are you okay?" Trevin asked as they both got up.

"Yeah," Alyssa said. "I just cut my finger."

"Do you want me to —?" Rubeus started as they walked into the kitchen.

"No!" Alyssa said, a little too quickly, pulling her hands to her chest. "It's just a paper cut. No big deal."

"Okay, well, it's getting late. We should probably get

going," Trevin said.

"What? I just put Jade down," Alyssa replied.

"It's fine. She can stay here," Michelle said. Rubeus shot her a look. "Or...you can stay too."

"Yeah, it could be like old times." Alyssa's eyes lit up. Rubeus and Trevin left the kitchen.

"Except I'm not staying up all night," Michelle added. She washed the knife and slipped it into the sink.

"You know what we *could* do?" Trevin asked as he came back to the kitchen doorway. The girls looked over.

"No," Rubeus said before Trevin could continue. "I'm not playing."

Trevin rolled his eyes. "Why not?" he asked as they all joined him in the living room.

"Because we're not twelve," Rubeus replied. "We're too old for that."

"No, we're not," Trevin stated. "I'm three hundred twenty-three, and I still love playing."

"What about a card game?" Alyssa asked, not wanting to see them fight.

"I'm not playing *any* games," Rubeus commented.

"Yeah, you are, and I know just what to get," Trevin said. "I'll be right back." He disappeared and returned a few minutes later with a black box.

"Is that what I think it is?" Alyssa asked. Trevin gave her a smile as he went into the dining room.

"What is it?" Michelle inquired.

"A messed up card game," Alyssa answered.

"Well, since *some* of you are worried about age-appropriate games, this one is for a mature audience only," Trevin said.

"Still not playing," Rubeus stated as he flipped through

a magazine.

"Come on, it's not fun with three people," Alyssa begged. She nudged Michelle to get her to help.

"You should have thought of that before everyone left," Rubeus responded.

"They're too old," Trevin said. "They wouldn't approve."

"Couldn't you do just one game?" Michelle asked. "I'd like to see what it's about."

Rubeus sighed. "One game." He reluctantly got up.

"Sweet," Trevin said. Everyone sat at the dining room table. Trevin went over the rules as Alyssa dealt the cards out. It didn't take long before everyone was laughing and having a good time. "Told ya you'd enjoy it."

"It's a good distraction," Michelle said, looking through her cards. Rubeus looked over at her. It took her a minute before she noticed. "What?"

"You just have a glow to you," Rubeus noticed as he moved some of her hair behind her ear.

Alyssa looked up and noticed her necklace wasn't there. She lightly bumped her under the table with her foot. Michelle glanced over and saw Alyssa casually rub her neck. Her heart skipped a beat as she looked back at Rubeus and smiled at him.

"Anyone thirsty?" Alyssa asked.

"I could go for some wine," Trevin said.

"I'll get it," Michelle said. "Red or white?"

"Red," Trevin said.

Michelle was about to get up and remembered that she was showing now, and disappeared instead. Alyssa looked down at the floor and saw the necklace. She put her foot on it and dragged it to her. She held her palm down towards the floor, and the necklace floated into her hand.

"I'm gonna go help her," Alyssa stated. She slipped the necklace into her pocket as she got up.

"They've been acting kind of odd." Rubeus watched Alyssa disappear into the kitchen before looking at his brother.

"I haven't noticed," Trevin replied, shuffling through his cards.

Alyssa found Michelle in the kitchen. "Wow, you're really showing," Alyssa whispered.

"I know," Michelle said. Alyssa put the necklace back on her. "How did it come off?"

"I don't know, but you're fine now," Alyssa answered. Michelle grabbed three wine glasses as Alyssa pulled out a bottle of red wine. "I'll take them out." Michelle poured it and grabbed herself a bottle of water. Alyssa took two glasses, and Michelle took her water and the other glass out.

"Where's yours?" Trevin asked.

"I don't want any," Michelle responded. "Besides, I'm going to bed soon."

There was a knock on the door. Rubeus started to get up to answer it.

"I got it." Michelle put her hand on his shoulder. "I'm already up." She went to the door and opened it. It was Aiden.

"Hey," he said as he peered inside to see if anyone else was around. "Can I ask you something?"

"I guess," Michelle said, crossing her arms.

"What do you think of Arixanna?" Aiden inquired.

"She's all right," Michelle responded. "From what I know of her."

"So, you wouldn't care if I asked her out?" Aiden asked.

"Why would I care?" Michelle questioned as she

stepped outside, closing the door.

"I don't know —" Aiden started.

"She's Rubeus's ex-girlfriend," Michelle interrupted.

"Never mind then." Aiden cringed.

"You do know we're married, right? So nobody should care," Michelle said, getting annoyed. "Besides, I think she likes you anyway."

"Really?" Aiden asked, his mood lifting.

"Mmmhmm," Michelle replied. "Have you had any luck locating the demon hunter?"

"No, not yet," Aiden said. "Everyone seems too distracted in finding out what I am. No one believes I'm human."

"Are you?" Michelle asked.

"You of all people should know," Aiden answered.

"Well, humans don't typically have special abilities like you," Michelle commented. "And I apparently don't know you. You kept this a secret."

"What else could I be?" Aiden questioned a little defensively. "Granted, there's no one else like me, but I don't know what else to tell you."

"I spent the first eighteen years of my life thinking I was human," Michelle retorted.

"Only Nerissa truly knows." Aiden started to say something else.

"I should get back inside before they start wondering."

Aiden nodded. "I guess I'll see you when it's your turn."

"Yeah," Michelle replied. He turned and went down the steps. "Hey…." He looked back at her. "You should go for it. With Arixanna." Aiden gave her a tight smile, turned back around, and left. Michelle went back inside.

"Who was at the door?" Rubeus asked.

"Aiden wanting my permission to go for Arixanna." Michelle rolled her eyes.

"What's he need your permission for?" Trevin asked.

"I don't know. I told him that she was *your* ex...," Michelle said, nodding at Rubeus. "...and that nobody cares."

"What about the demon hunter?" Alyssa inquired.

"Still no luck," Michelle said. "He said everyone seems to be more interested in if he's human or not, which he swears he is. He doesn't know what else he would be."

"I could ask Nerissa," Alyssa suggested.

"Because she'll tell you the truth," Rubeus commented. "Besides, the less she knows what we're doing, the better."

"She's the one that led us to him." Alyssa started.

"Right. Well, I'm going to bed," Michelle stated, hoping to avoid an argument between them. She gave Rubeus a quick kiss and went upstairs.

"I'm gonna make sure she's all right." Alyssa started to get up.

"I think I can handle that," Rubeus responded as he grabbed her arm and pulled her back. He left to go upstairs.

"He's right. You have been acting odd," Trevin stated. "What's going on?"

"What? Nothing," Alyssa lied.

"You're lying," Trevin said, studying her face. "Tell me."

"I can't," Alyssa said. "I promised I wouldn't tell anyone."

***

Michelle had taken the necklace off as soon as she went upstairs. She was in the bathroom in just her bra and underwear, looking at herself in profile. Michelle couldn't believe how much she was already showing, but demons only carried for six months. The nausea had pretty much phased out since she was in her second trimester.

She heard someone coming down the hall and quickly put the necklace back on. Her body immediately looked normal. Michelle grabbed her brush and started to brush her hair as Rubeus stuck his head in the bathroom.

"Are you okay?" he asked.

She set the brush down and turned. "Why wouldn't I be?" Michelle asked as she moved around him in the doorway.

"You haven't been acting quite like yourself lately." Rubeus had a worried expression.

"I have a lot on my mind, that's all," Michelle replied. She folded the covers on her side of the bed back. "I hope we find him soon."

"We will," Rubeus reassured her. He came up behind her and wrapped his arms around her. "Promise that's all?"

"Yeah," Michelle said. She twisted around and kissed him before he let her go and got into bed.

***

"You *cannot* say anything," Alyssa demanded. "Especially to Michelle or Rubeus."

Trevin said nothing. He was still in complete shock. They both looked over when they saw Rubeus come back downstairs. Trevin rested his elbow on the table and covered his mouth with his hand.

"Is she okay?" Alyssa asked.

"Not sick, is she?" Trevin let slip out. Alyssa kicked him. "Ow!"

"Just worried about everything," Rubeus said, giving him an odd look.

"Uh, you know, I'm suddenly really tired. I think I'm

gonna go too," Trevin said. He got up and quickly left the room. Rubeus gave Alyssa a questioning look.

"Maybe he had too much wine?" she suggested, shrugging as she got up, gathering the glasses.

"I'll get those," Rubeus said.

Alyssa set them back down and headed to bed. Once Rubeus was sure everyone was asleep, he disappeared and reappeared in the human realm, where it was early afternoon. It was towards the end of winter, but everyone was still bundled up. There was a fresh blanket of snow on the ground, with more on the way. There was always one last storm before spring hit.

Rubeus debated going to see Remus or his father but decided not to. Instead, he headed towards the lake. Rubeus had been having this feeling that someone, or something, was watching him. No matter where he went, he couldn't shake the feeling, almost like it was attached to him. He had an idea of who it was but wanted to be certain.

People quickly moved out of his way as he walked down the street. Demons stood out more in the wintertime since they were used to the cold. He didn't need a coat. Rubeus approached the lake. The invisible field rippled with energy as he stepped through it. There was a dark figure at the end of the dock wearing a cloak.

"I was wondering how long it would take you to find me," the figure said. "I've been on you for a while." The figure flickered in and out of existence, telling Rubeus that he wasn't really there.

"Whatever you've come back for, leave Michelle and everyone else out of it," Rubeus said.

"Well, I'm technically only here for you and her," he replied.

"I'll kill you," Rubeus threatened.

The image of the demon hunter smiled. "You're lucky I'm not really here," the demon hunter stated. "I'd tear you limb from limb right now, and then I'd finally be able to get close enough to get a grip on Michelle."

"You'll never get close enough," Rubeus said confidently.

"Only because my scout hasn't been able to be around her long enough. But that's about to change," the demon hunter said. "I'll be seeing you real soon." The image blinked out.

"Aiden," Rubeus said. "I knew it." He disappeared.

CHAPTER 26

"You wanted to see me?" Arixanna asked as she walked into Rubeus's office. He was leaning against his desk, so she stopped a few feet in front of him.

"Where have you been?" Rubeus questioned as he folded his arms.

"I've been busy with Aiden," Arixanna responded, feeling the irritation from him. "You know that."

"You must have a lot of information for me then," Rubeus replied.

"No, not yet," Arixanna said. "There's been no luck with the demon hunter either."

"Maybe it's because you're not focusing on the mission," Rubeus commented.

"Excuse me?" Arixanna asked, clearly offended.

"Aiden stopped by about a week ago, asking Michelle if he could ask you out."

"A week ago?" Arixanna asked. "Why are you bringing it up now?"

"I haven't been able to get ahold of you," Rubeus stated. "Probably because you've been too busy with Aiden."

"It's my rotation with him," Arixanna snapped. "So, yeah."

"Then tell me how Michelle got more information out of him within a couple of minutes than the entire few weeks you've been with him," Rubeus asked. Arixanna breathed in to answer. "I'll tell you how. It's because you're too busy trying to get in his pants to complete the mission at hand."

"That's *not* what I've been doing," Arixanna rebutted, getting angry. "Besides, why do you even care what I do in my personal time?"

"I *don't* care what you do," Rubeus said. "But I do expect you to do your job, which you're clearly not. Your rotation is over."

"What? I still have two more weeks," Arixanna pleaded.

"Not anymore. I've already told Sven that he's taking over," Rubeus responded. "I also want you to stay away from him."

"You can't do that."

"He's dangerous," Rubeus stated.

"Just because you don't like him doesn't make him dangerous," Arixanna replied. "You don't have the right or the power to tell me who I can hang around."

"It's a matter of your safety," Rubeus said.

"I don't need you to protect me—I haven't for years," Arixanna retorted. "I can handle my own safety." She walked away from him.

"Arixanna!" Rubeus called after her.

She ignored him and disappeared down the hallway to the door.

CHAPTER 27

Sven didn't waste any time once he started his rotation with Aiden. He immediately took him to the other side of the realm to see if the area was accessible again. Seeing that it was, they started to do a sweep of the area.

"I thought your area was the section along the other side of the banana trees," Aiden said.

"It is, but I wanted to see if this place really was here like Rubeus claimed," Sven replied. "This should have been the first place to look."

"Well, he did let you choose your own section. It's not his fault everyone chose not to come here," Aiden commented. "We should probably get to yours. I don't want to be blamed for stepping out of line."

"You wouldn't get the blame," Sven said.

"I'm pretty sure I would," Aiden stated. "He doesn't like me." He started into the banana trees.

"Well, you are my daughter's ex," Sven responded.

"*You're* her father?" Aiden stopped and looked back at him. "She told me he died."

"She didn't know until a couple of years ago," Sven said.

"So, she has relations with all the elders?" Aiden

inquired. "No wonder she has a seat of power."

"She has no blood ties to Arixanna," Sven replied. "She only got a seat because Remus chose her to replace him, but she's a pureblood—she would have become one eventually. I would have chosen her myself when the time came." They continued through the trees until they got to the other side.

"Is Remus related to her too?" Aiden questioned as they continued scanning the area.

"Not by blood. He's Rubeus's grandfather."

"What happened to him? Did he die?" Aiden asked.

"He sacrificed his power in order for the new Apostle to be born," Sven explained. "Losing one's power, regardless of how, makes you human. He's now living in the human realm where Michelle was."

"So, he can be in the sunlight now?" Aiden asked.

"Yes," Sven said.

"That doesn't make sense," Aiden thought. "I thought your DNA was changed, not your power."

"They're linked together in some ways. Changing one can change the other," Sven said. "It becomes quite complicated if you try to get to the root of it. Only Nerissa truly understands it."

"I keep hearing you guys talk about her like she's this almighty God."

"I wouldn't go that far, but in a way, she is," Sven replied. "She was the head witch elder when the others were still alive. Now she's the last. She's been around since the beginning and created everything you see before you—with the others' help, of course. She's very powerful."

"If she wants to be rid of you, why doesn't she just kill you?" Aiden asked.

"She can't physically kill us. It would go against the

agreement," Sven stated. Aiden stopped. "If anyone breaks any part of the agreement that was made millennia ago, the Apostle will kill them. Nerissa has a way of manipulating events into working in her favor. She has the ability to see the possible outcomes of different events and chooses which path she wants a specific one to follow." They continued their way through some brush.

"I guess the demon hunter wasn't an accident," Aiden said. He looked at his watch. He was surprised at the time.

"I'm afraid it wasn't," Sven said. "That's enough of this for today. I think we made good progress."

CHAPTER 28

"What are you doing? It's my rotation," Michelle said. She and Rubeus were standing just inside the foyer, waiting for Aiden to show up.

"You're no longer part of it," Rubeus replied.

"You've gotta be kidding," Michelle said angrily. "There's nothing for you to worry about. I've told you that."

"That's not why I'm taking you out of it," Rubeus snapped as he gripped something in his pocket. "You just have to trust me on this."

"You keep saying that. I need to know why," Michelle said, starting to worry.

Rubeus wrapped his arms around her. "Just know that I love you, and I'm only doing this to protect you," Rubeus responded.

Michelle felt her power diminish as he pulled away on the verge of tears. Michelle saw a gold bracelet on her wrist.

"No," Michelle whispered as tears formed.

"I don't want you to follow me."

"Don't do this," Michelle pleaded as tears started to fall.

"I'm sorry," he said as he went outside.

Aiden was waiting in front of the steps. Michelle

ran outside. Rubeus looked up at her one last time before disappearing with Aiden. Michelle fell to her knees, crying while trying to pull the bracelet off.

***

Rubeus took Aiden to the west side of the realm.

"What are we doing here?" Aiden asked, crossing his arms. "And I thought it was Michelle's turn."

Rubeus turned to him. "I don't want her involved in this. You and I both know you're the scout."

"What? That's ludicrous," Aiden said, shocked. Rubeus stepped up to him and picked what appeared to be a mole off the back of his hairline. "Ow!" Aiden looked at it as his eyes briefly flashed. "That's…impossible."

"It makes perfect sense," Rubeus stated. "That second sight of yours identifies us for the demon hunter, and this device sends him the info." He crushed it between his fingers.

"I swear to you I had no idea."

"You wouldn't think to check yourself. He was counting on that," Rubeus replied. "The demon hunter's been on me for a while. I just hope he hasn't gotten Michelle yet."

"How do you know that?" Aiden asked.

"I can't explain it, I just know," Rubeus said. "I brought you here because this is where I believe the demon hunter is. I just need you to confirm it, and then you can get back to your life in the human realm."

"You can't stop him," Aiden said.

"No, but I can delay him long enough to get you out of here so he can't get to Michelle."

"That still won't keep her safe. Demon hunters can shapeshift," Aiden informed him. "All he needs is some of your skin and blood."

"He's as good as dead then," Rubeus commented. "Go

do your thing."

Aiden started walking around. He stopped when he saw the cave. He closed his eyes and concentrated, activating his second sight.

"In there," Aiden said. "There are two energy signatures, one witch and the other neither witch nor demonic. I've seen the one before, back at the club, where my sister read fortunes."

"Which one?" Rubeus asked.

"I think you know which," Aiden answered. "That's why I thought you and Trevin were part of it. My sister was locked up in a trunk."

"He must have impersonated her," Rubeus thought out loud. "That's how he got a hold of me."

They heard someone laugh. "Very clever," the demon hunter said. They looked up and saw a dark figure perched on top of the cave.

"Now's a good time to get me out of here," Aiden said through the corner of his mouth.

"I don't think so," the demon hunter said. Energy whipped out and hit Aiden, throwing him into the surf. "He's still of use to me. I told you I'd see you soon. Are you here to surrender?"

"Not without a fight," Rubeus said. The demon hunter smiled as he leapt into the air.

***

Trevin cut the bracelet off Michelle with the plyers they had taken from the chop shop a few years ago.

"Why would he do that?" Alyssa asked.

"He didn't want me to follow him," Michelle said. "I think he knows where the demon hunter is and went to face him."

"But that's suicide," Alyssa said. Michelle looked away.

***

"It's been a while since I've had this much fun," the demon hunter said as he approached Rubeus. Rubeus tried to get up but couldn't. He was injured badly and wasn't healing himself. "I bet Michelle will put up an even better one. Females have always had more power."

"You won't get the chance to find out," Rubeus said as the demon hunter picked him up.

"You don't think?" the demon hunter asked. "Nerissa informed me about your blood and how toxic it is. She gave me a concoction to keep it from affecting me."

"Nerissa?" Rubeus asked.

"Don't sound so surprised," the demon hunter replied. "But know that I'll be going after her next." Rubeus felt truly defeated. "Now to take your form," Rubeus screamed as the demon hunter dug his claws into his shoulder and ripped the flesh from him.

***

Aiden finally came to. He pushed up onto his knees and looked around. He saw someone walking towards him.

"Let's get out of here," Rubeus said.

Aiden looked around before standing. "What happened to the demon hunter?" Aiden asked, a little suspicious.

"He won't be bothering us for a while," Rubeus responded.

Aiden brought up his second sight. "You're not Rubeus," Aiden stated. "Is he dead?"

"He's very resilient," the demon hunter commented. "He's on his way out, though."

"What do you need me for then?" Aiden asked. "You

can get to her now."

The demon hunter grabbed hold of him. "They need someone to place blame on."

"I'll tell them as soon we get back," Aiden threatened.

"And I'll let them know that you were really created specifically to help my kind hunt them down."

"That's not true," Aiden said.

"There's nothing special about the demon's aura. That gift, as you call it, helps you distinguish which demons are purebloods, that's all," the demon hunter informed him, confirming Rubeus's theory. "I wanna have some fun. Let's see how long it takes them to figure it out."

He disappeared with Aiden.

CHAPTER 29

"They're back," Alyssa said, looking out the window.

Michelle looked up. "Both of them?" She rushed to the window.

"Yeah," Alyssa answered.

Michelle ran outside, down the steps, and into his arms, causing Rubeus to fall. Aiden looked away, not able to watch.

"I thought I was never going to see you again," Michelle said as they both stood. "What happened? Did you see him?" Trevin and Alyssa stepped outside.

"We don't have to worry about him anymore," Rubeus said.

"You killed a demon hunter?" Alyssa questioned, suspicious.

Rubeus looked up at her. "No," Rubeus responded, making eye contact. "He's just severely injured and won't be coming after anyone for quite a while."

The demon hunter continued to fool them for the next few days, but he started to have trouble keeping his disguise. Cuts and bruises started to form on his skin. He soon realized that the concoction Nerissa had given him only temporarily stopped the effects of Rubeus's blood. If he wanted Michelle, he was going to have to make his move soon.

"Are you sure you're feeling all right?" Michelle asked. "You've been kinda off lately."

The five of them were all in the dining room. Aiden, Trevin, and Alyssa were sitting at the table. Rubeus was flipping through a book, and Michelle was leaning against the table beside him.

"I've just been a little tired," Rubeus said.

Michelle went to touch him, but he moved slightly away from her. She glanced down and saw an open cut on his forearm. "I see," Michelle said as she turned from him. "I know you like to feel normal sometimes, but you should really take care of that. It looks infected." She started to sit down with the others.

"Normal?" Rubeus asked, looking over at her. Michelle stopped as Trevin, Alyssa, and she exchanged glances. "What do you mean by that?"

"Well, you hardly ever get injured, so when you do, it gives you a sense of normalcy," Michelle explained.

Rubeus glanced down at his forearm and then back to her. "Right," he said slowly, still not understanding. "Sorry, I'm just not thinking straight today. I think I'm gonna go lay down."

Rubeus started to walk away, but Michelle grabbed the wrist of the injured arm and brought his forearm up. Alyssa started to protest, but Trevin nudged her from under the table. Michelle licked the blood off his forearm while he gave her an odd look.

"How long?" Michelle asked, spitting it out.

"Excuse me?" Rubeus responded.

"How long have you had him?" Michelle demanded as she threw his arm down.

"I don't —," he started.

"Rubeus would've *never* let me get close enough," Michelle said sternly. His eyes twitched as he grabbed ahold of her. She tried to push away from him as Trevin and Alyssa started to get up. His grip tightened on her.

"Not another step, or I'll skin her alive," Rubeus threatened. They sat back down.

"How long?" Michelle asked again.

"Why? Worried we got too close?" Rubeus inquired as he ran his hand down the side of her face. She spit in his face, and he grabbed the back of her hair. She flinched. "It's only been a couple of days. I was hoping this would've lasted longer." He saw movement and spun her around, twisting her arm. She cried out. Black smoke surrounded him as he changed into his true form. His entire body was pitch black, making it hard to really see what he looked like. He had two horns on his head that curled back like a ram and a tail with spikes on the end of it.

"What have you done with Rubeus?" Trevin asked.

"You needn't worry about that," the demon hunter said, gazing at him with his horrifyingly pure white eyes.

"You killed him," Michelle struggled.

"He wasn't dead when I left, but he might be now. He put up a good fight. It was the most fun I've had in millennia. But enough chit chat. Are you ready to join him?" He breathed her in. "I do love the smell of fear on demons." Black wings extended outward. "None of this would have been possible without your help, Aiden. We fooled them longer than I thought we would." Michelle gave Aiden a shocked look. The demon hunter jumped into the air with Michelle, broke through the roof of the manor, and flew off.

Trevin grabbed ahold of Aiden. "You knew this whole

time?" Trevin demanded through gritted teeth.

"Yes, but he threatened to hurt Michelle if I didn't keep quiet," Aiden said. "I'm sorry."

"He's going to kill her regardless." Trevin pushed him away.

"Well, what are we supposed to do now?" Alyssa asked.

"Get them back," Trevin responded. "And find a way to kill him."

"How? No one knows how to kill a demon hunter," Aiden reiterated.

"We could ask the elders," Alyssa suggested. "They may know. They were around when they initially appeared."

"It's a good start. Go to Nerissa, and I'll ask Camilla and the others," Trevin said. Alyssa disappeared.

"What do you want me to do?" Aiden asked.

"Stay out of our way," Trevin said. "You've done enough already."

CHAPTER 30

The demon hunter landed on the other side of the realm near a cave by the beach and dragged Michelle in. It was a lot larger inside than it appeared. Hundreds of cages lined the walls. He took her past them all. The cave branched off into several tunnels. He took the one farthest to the right.

"Do you have a name?" Michelle asked.

"You won't live long enough to remember it."

"That's not true. You would have killed me already," Michelle stated.

"I like to play with my food first," the demon hunter replied. "But if it's that important, it's Dracul."

He stopped by a large cell, which was slightly furnished. A prison style bunk bed was to the right. Rubeus was on the bottom bed. Michelle saw him, and her heart skipped a beat.

Dracul opened the cell door and threw her in. She slammed into the wall and fell to the floor. Michelle felt a sharp pain in her lower back and then nothing. He closed the door and walked away. Michelle pushed herself up with her hands and tried to stand, but realized she couldn't feel her legs. Her body wasn't healing from it, so she could only assume the damaged nerves affected the connection to the baby too.

Michelle looked over at Rubeus, who hadn't stirred at all. Michelle dragged herself to him and up onto a chair beside the bed. She could barely stand the look of him. Rubeus was very pale and cold to the touch. Skin was torn off his right shoulder, exposing the muscle. There were gashes and bruises all over him. Michelle could only imagine how many bones were broken. Some of Rubeus's hair was caked in blood. There was a deep cut on his cheek that went down to the bone. Michelle nudged him but got no kind of response.

"You've gotta be in there somewhere," Michelle whispered. She placed her hand on his forehead, closed her eyes, and pushed into his mind, looking for some kind of life. After a few minutes of searching, Michelle was about to give up when she finally felt a small pulse of existence deep within his subconscious.

There was white all around her as she continued to walk across the expanse towards the small life force she felt. Random images of Rubeus's childhood flashed in front of her and disappeared just as quickly. Michelle heard laughter as two boys appeared and ran past her. They vanished into the nothingness. An echoed scream caused Michelle to stop. She looked around until something flickered in her peripheral. It was McCain—his body was on fire. Others were rushing around, trying to figure out what to do. A young Rubeus stood in the background, staring at the fire. He had to be about ten. There was an older man kneeling beside him, talking to him. *Only you can stop that fire. Concentrate!* The young Rubeus looked at the man, who Michelle finally recognized as Trevin. His eyes were wide and fearful. As he closed them, the images disappeared. There was a man sitting off in the distance. Michelle couldn't tell if it was real or just another image. As she got closer, she saw it was Rubeus, in a meditation pose.

His body was translucent.

"I knew you had to be here somewhere," Michelle said as she sat in front of him.

"What are you doing here?" Rubeus asked, keeping his eyes closed.

"I had to know if you were alive," Michelle answered. "Why aren't you healing yourself?"

"I don't want him to know I can," Rubeus responded as he opened his eyes. "It's taking everything I have not to."

"You're gonna die if you don't," Michelle pleaded. "You're in really bad shape. You're cold to the touch." She reached out to touch him as tears formed, but her hand went right through him.

"I took care of the life-threatening injuries," Rubeus reassured her. "I'm cold because I stopped my blood from circulating."

"I don't understand," Michelle said.

"Another unique ability the enzyme gives me," Rubeus explained. "It's sort of a defense mechanism. But why are you here? Did he get you?"

"He was posing as you," Michelle replied. "Can't you teleport out?"

"I've tried, but once he's latched on, it's impossible to get away from him," Rubeus said. She had no response. "Are you okay? Did he hurt you?"

"I can't feel my legs," Michelle confessed. She felt the pain in him from her answer.

"You realize I can't heal you," Rubeus responded. "It would bring too much of me back."

"I recall telling you I didn't need you to heal me every time I got hurt," Michelle said, trying to make light of it.

"Paralysis is a little more severe than a burnt hand,"

Rubeus stated. "You need to go. This contact is becoming too much."

"But —," Michelle started.

"I'll find a way to get you out, I promise," Rubeus reassured. He started pushing her out of his mind. "Be ready."

Michelle's body started moving backwards. "No, wait!" Michelle yelled, but it was too late.

Michelle opened her eyes and took her hand from him. She slid out of the chair and took his hand in hers as tears slid down her face.

CHAPTER 31

Trevin stood before the elders at City Hall. They all looked like they had given up hope when he told them the demon hunter had Michelle and Rubeus.

"So there's absolutely nothing that can be done?" Trevin asked in disbelief. "None of you know anything?"

"There was nothing ever written about demon hunters," Camilla stated. "It was thought that they were all taken care of in the war, so nothing was ever documented on them."

"That war took place a couple of hundred years before any of us were born," Sven added.

"Remus and Bane were alive during that time," Arixanna stated. "Bane is dead, and Remus no longer has any power."

"He can still help," Alyssa said as she appeared in City Hall. She approached them.

"What did you find out?" Trevin asked as she stopped beside him.

"She won't tell me anything," Alyssa replied.

"Of course not. She wants us extinct," Sven responded.

"Let's go see Remus then," Trevin suggested. They disappeared and reappeared in the mansion. They found him sitting in the living room. Remus stood up when he saw them. "We need your help."

"I'll do my best," Remus said, seeing the desperation in their eyes.

"Do you know anything about demon hunters and how to kill them?" Trevin asked.

Remus stiffened at the mention of it. "They were all banished in the great war," Remus answered. "It's been so long they should've died from starvation by now."

"One is still alive," Alyssa informed him. "It has Michelle and Rubeus."

Remus sighed and turned away from them. "What does he look like?" Remus inquired.

"Dark as night —," Trevin started.

"Dracul," Remus interrupted, not needing any more information. "He was the most dangerous."

"Do you know how to kill him?" Alyssa asked.

"There's only one who knows how to deal with a demon hunter," Remus stated as he turned back to them. "He never wrote it down because we were sure we got rid of them all."

"Who?" Trevin asked.

Remus said nothing.

"You've got to be kidding," Alyssa said.

"I'm sorry, but if you want to save them, you'll have to resurrect him," Remus said.

CHAPTER 32

People started screaming as Dracul wreaked havoc in the space between the realms, searching for Nerissa. A thick stream of energy slammed into him, causing him to fall to his knees.

"How did you get here?" Nerissa demanded, walking out of the castle. She stopped several feet out from him.

"I've been here before, remember?" Dracul stated as he stood.

Nerissa narrowed her eyes at him. "You look horrible," Nerissa responded. "Must have been something you ate."

"You tricked me," Dracul said, taking a step towards her. "You said this would keep his blood from attacking me." He smashed the flask he had pulled out.

"You're still alive, aren't you?" Nerissa responded. Dracul said nothing. "I never said it was a permanent solution."

He quickly closed the distance and grabbed ahold of her. "I should tear you apart."

"You could," Nerissa stated, showing no fear. "But then how will you get a constant supply of the suppressant? Only I know how to make it." He slowly sat her down. "Now, did you finish them?"

"They're both as good as dead," Dracul said, more calm.

"Let me know when they are, and I'll give you another dose," Nerissa said as she handed him a very small vial. He drank the potion, only feeling slightly better. "Now get out of here. And don't ever come here attacking my people again."

Dracul snarled at her before disappearing.

CHAPTER 33

"You must be desperate if you're bringing *me* back," Bane commented as he came into the living room in the mansion, buttoning the cuffs on his shirt. He looked around at his surroundings. "What are we doing *here*?"

"This is where I stay now," Remus said. He started to shift the logs in the fireplace with a fire poker.

"You're human? I can't do anything to help you with that," Bane replied.

"That's not why you're here," Trevin said.

Bane noticed him and Alyssa.

"Dracul is back," Remus stated.

"Nerissa's plan worked then," Bane thought. "All my attempts to stop her were for nothing."

"You've never made any attempts to stop her," Remus accused. "You've been working with her, trying to get rid of Rubeus and Michelle. All you ever cared about was keeping your place as head elder."

"That's not why I wanted rid of them. Take a step back and look at the big picture, you fool," Bane rebutted. "She wanted them to survive to bring Dracul back. Only then would she have the power to rid herself of us. Nerissa foresaw all of this. I wanted them gone so her visions *wouldn't* come to pass."

"That's great. You're a fucking saint," Trevin responded. "You're the only one with the information we need. How can we get rid of him?"

"The best way would be to open a rift, but not even Nerissa has that kind of power," Bane said.

"Then how did you get them in one, to begin with?" Alyssa questioned.

"The creation of McCain caused the rift, and we pushed them into it," Bane answered.

"Is there any other way?" Trevin asked.

"The next best thing would be to imprison him on the west coast with a force field the length of the realm," Bane stated. "It takes a lot of power to create a field that big. Seeing as you're short on elders, I don't see that happening."

"How many do you need?" Alyssa asked.

"All the elders, I would imagine," Bane contemplated. "There's only one witch elder, and what…three demon elders?"

"There's still five," Trevin said, confident his brother and Michelle were still alive.

"But Dracul has Rubeus and Michelle," Alyssa replied.

"They're as good as dead then," Bane said. "There's no way to stop him. Nerissa has won."

"We don't know that for sure," Trevin said optimistically. "Dracul even said Rubeus wasn't dead."

"If they can get free, you'd be able to create the field," Bane said. "Just Rubeus has enough power as five elders. Michelle, being female, would have double that."

"Then let's get them," Alyssa said.

"It's a suicide mission," Bane stated. "You'll never make it close enough."

"We're not giving up," Trevin said.

"There must be something you could do," Alyssa implored.

"You're wasting your time trying to convince him to help," Trevin commented. "He only cares about himself. Come on." Trevin and Alyssa disappeared.

Remus turned to Bane. "She's your granddaughter," Remus pleaded.

"Using blood ties won't help your cause," Bane responded. "Look what I did to my own daughters."

"Then make up for it with Michelle. You owe her that," Remus said. "You owe them both."

Bane sighed as he looked away. "I may be able to distract him long enough for them to get enough distance to teleport out of his reach," Bane said softly. "Is he still on the west side?"

"I believe so, but I've not been to the demonic realm for quite some time now."

"I'll see what I can do then," Bane said. He disappeared.

CHAPTER 34

Dracul appeared back in the cave. The small amount of the potion Nerissa had given him really didn't do too much. He took a knee, trying to regain some of his strength.

Michelle looked over at him. "For someone who can't die, you certainly look like death."

He looked over at her. "I'm not immortal," Dracul replied. "I was engineered to be difficult to kill." He stood up. "It appears that my life is at risk as long as you two are alive."

"Weren't you planning on killing us anyway?" Michelle commented.

"Two purebloods really aren't worth my time," Dracul stated. "I only went after you because Nerissa wanted me to, but his blood is slowly killing me, and only Nerissa has what I need to prolong my life."

"You get what you deserve putting your trust in her," Michelle responded.

Dracul ripped the cell door off its hinges and grabbed ahold of her, lifting her off the ground. "And you will be the first to die." Dracul shielded his eyes from the brilliant flash of light that came from inside the cell. Energy slammed into him. He dropped Michelle as he went flying into the far wall.

Rubeus caught Michelle and disappeared. He

reappeared outside the cave, which was as far as he could teleport because of the hold Dracul had. Rubeus sat Michelle down and healed her. Once she was steady on her legs, they took off running. They heard Dracul yell from inside the cave.

"No fucking way," Michelle gasped as she skidded to a stop just as she hit a clearing. Rubeus slammed into her, unable to stop in time, causing them both to fall over. He looked where she was, eyes widening. Rubeus jumped to his feet and immediately pulled her up and behind him. They heard Dracul crashing through the forest behind them. He turned and looked back, not knowing who the bigger threat was.

"I'm not here to hurt you...this time," Bane promised.

"Yeah, right," Rubeus responded.

"Get behind me," Bane ordered. "Or would you rather face Dracul?"

"I don't know which is worse," Michelle admitted.

"I'd rather take my chances with Bane," Rubeus decided. He pulled Michelle with him and got behind Bane.

"I'll distract him so you can get away," Bane said.

"We can't travel anywhere," Rubeus informed him. "He locks onto it."

"You just need enough distance between you," Bane explained.

"Why are you helping us?" Michelle asked.

"Because I want Nerissa to fail more than I want you dead," Bane answered. "Now go."

Rubeus and Michelle took off running again. "Do you think we can trust him?" Michelle asked.

"Absolutely not," Rubeus said. "But we at least know he can be killed."

"Yeah, he just doesn't stay dead," Michelle replied.

Bane finally caught up to them just as they reached the cabin on the west side.

"How far does his reach go?" Michelle inquired.

"The entire coast," Bane responded. "That's why we sealed this side off once they were all banished." They went inside the cabin.

"How are you even back?" Rubeus asked.

"Your brother must have more power than he lets on," Bane said. "I was resurrected. I know Remus couldn't have done it."

"Alyssa," Michelle stated.

"I doubt it. Even Nerissa doesn't have that kind of power."

"She's the new Apostle," Michelle informed.

"Why did they do it?" Rubeus asked.

"Desperate times call for desperate measures," Bane said. "I'm the only one with the knowledge to rid our realm of him."

"Well, how do we kill him?" Michelle questioned.

"You can't kill a demon hunter in any traditional way. Nerissa made them to be highly resistant to our power. You'll have to create a field and trap him on this side. It takes a lot of power to do it, but since you both are purebloods, it will be enough."

"You *can* kill him," Michelle said. "He told me himself he isn't immortal. He's only after us now because Nerissa has something to keep Rubeus's blood from killing him."

"So that's what he meant. Clever witch," Bane thought out loud. "She found a way to rid herself of the demon hunter after he rids her of you two."

"What did you do to get him to back off?" Rubeus asked.

"That's something you don't need to worry about," Bane stated. "You should go while you still can. You'll be able to teleport home once you get out of the brush."

Rubeus went outside. Michelle started to follow, then stopped. "Hold on a minute." She went back inside. "I don't know why you're doing this, but thank you."

Bane turned to her. "I have a lot to make up for," Bane replied. "My previous actions towards you or my daughters were never personal. I hope you can one day understand that."

"I'm starting to," Michelle said.

She embraced him in a hug, startling him. After a moment's hesitation, he embraced her back.

"We need to go," Rubeus said as he came back in. He stopped short when he saw them. Michelle let Bane go and went outside. Rubeus and Bane made eye contact briefly before Rubeus went back out. "What was that about?"

"We came to an understanding," Michelle said. "He *is* my grandfather."

"Yeah, unfortunately, we don't get to choose," Rubeus replied. "Let's get out of here."

As they pushed through more brush, gold dust flew up into the air. Rubeus sneezed as he accidentally inhaled it. Michelle looked back at him. He fell to his knees and grabbed his head. She started to make her way back to him, but he put his hand out to stop her. "Keep going."

"I'm not gonna leave you," Michelle said. "What's wrong?"

"It'd be best if you kept running and stayed away from me," Rubeus said. He looked up at her, his eyes completely dilated and glowing. Michelle faltered and took a step back. "Bane did something. I can't...." He started to lose the familiar look she always saw in his eyes. "Go!"

Michelle turned and vanished.

"Kill her," someone whispered. Rubeus stood, eyes still glowing. "And anyone that stands in your way." Rubeus disappeared.

Michelle skidded to a halt as Rubeus appeared in front of her. She dove out of the way as he threw lightning at her.

"No," Michelle whispered as she stood. Trevin and Alyssa saw them and started to run towards them. Michelle looked over. "Stop!" she yelled at them. "Don't come over here!" They stopped in their tracks as Rubeus formed more lightning.

"What's he doing?" Alyssa whispered.

Rubeus whipped around and threw the lightning towards Trevin and Alyssa. It slammed into Alyssa. She cried out as she fell to the ground.

"Alyssa!" Michelle yelled.

"Have you gone mad!" Trevin yelled as he knelt beside her.

More lightning soared towards them. Michelle appeared in front of them and deflected it.

"I don't know what happened to him, but he's turned against us," Michelle said.

A stream of lightning came towards them. Michelle formed lightning and emitted it at him. The energies collided in a brilliant flash of light.

"Get out of here and warn the others."

Trevin picked up Alyssa and disappeared.

Rubeus pushed a surge of energy towards Michelle and pushed through her attack. It crashed into her, knocking her down. Rubeus jumped into the air and started to barrage her with attacks. Michelle quickly put herself in a bubble before the first one hit as she healed from the lightning.

"Whatever this is, you've gotta fight it!"

He landed by her head. She dropped the field around her and quickly got up as she tried to capture him in a bubble, but he disappeared. Michelle looked around, waiting, only to see him reappear. She quickly turned around and threw a punch, but he blocked it. They started to fight hand to hand. Rubeus was too quick for her to try and counterattack. All she could do was block, and she was barely fast enough for that.

CHAPTER 35

Trevin rushed into City Hall and laid Alyssa down on one of the benches near the receptionist's desk.

"What's going on?" Arixanna inquired.

"Rubeus has completely lost it," Trevin said. "He attacked us and is fighting Michelle right now."

"What?" Sven asked as he and the other elders came out of one of the side rooms.

"He's turned on us," Trevin said in a panic.

"How did this happen?" Camilla asked. Trevin shook his head.

Alyssa started to come to. "What happened?" she asked, rubbing her head.

"Rubeus hit you," Trevin answered.

She sat up, remembering. "We have to help Michelle."

"How?" Trevin asked. "He's too powerful for any of us to fight. Michelle's the only one with a chance."

"Well, he can't fight all of us at once," Alyssa responded.

The elders looked at each other. "You've obviously never seen him fight," Arixanna said.

***

Rubeus knocked Michelle to the ground and stood over her. She looked up at him while trying to catch her breath.

"This isn't you," Michelle pleaded. "Please."

Rubeus formed fire in his hands, but she grabbed a handful of sand and threw it in his face just as he prepared to attack. The fire vanished from his hands as he stumbled back, trying to get the sand from his eyes. Michelle disappeared while she had the chance. He quickly recovered and looked around to find her gone. He disappeared.

Michelle went to the human realm to the mansion. She burst through the doors, startling Remus and Ryan.

"You're alive!" Remus exclaimed as he met her in the hall.

"What's going on?" Ryan asked as he joined them. "What happened to you?"

Michelle was covered with sweat, dirt, and blood. Her clothes were torn and scorched.

"Rubeus," Michelle started, still trying to catch her breath. "Something was cast on him or put on him—I don't know, but I need to fix it. Do you know of any spells or potions that can?"

"I'm afraid I would need to know exactly what caused the change," Remus admitted.

Michelle closed her eyes and let out a heavy sigh as she fell to her knees. "I need some kind of help," Michelle said as tears started to form. "I can't beat him. I'm not strong enough."

Ryan knelt before her. "Yes, you can. Don't think for a moment that just because he's physically stronger than you that you can't do it. You're a female pureblood, which means *you* are stronger. You wield more power than he could ever imagine."

"That doesn't matter. He's too fast for me to get to," Michelle complained. "I can't even get a bubble around him."

She looked down at the floor.

"Then let him get to *you*," Ryan said. "Remind him who you are and what you're capable of."

"Remind him," Michelle whispered. She looked up at them. "I think I may know how to get him back."

CHAPTER 36

People screamed as they ran for cover. Rubeus was storming through the city looking for Michelle.

"Where is she?" he demanded as he grabbed ahold of someone.

"I don't know. I haven't seen her," the man said with fear in his eyes. "I swear."

"Hey!" Trevin yelled as he threw lightning at Rubeus. It hit the dirt beside him.

Rubeus looked down at the scorched earth and let the man go. He turned and faced Trevin and started towards him. Trevin emitted a stream of energy at him. Rubeus countered it with his own. He quickly pushed through Trevin's and hit him with it. Trevin fell to the ground.

Michelle appeared and knelt beside him. "Are you okay?" Michelle asked. Trevin nodded as he propped up on his elbows. "And Alyssa?"

"She's fine."

"I think I know what to do —" Michelle stated.

"There you are," Rubeus said.

"Give 'em hell," Trevin said.

Michelle looked over at Rubeus and stood as Trevin disappeared.

"Miss me?" Michelle asked.

"Hardly," Rubeus responded.

Ryan appeared with Remus by the other elders, Trevin, and Alyssa on the steps of City Hall. Everyone else was safely indoors, with a few watching from the safety of their windows. Rubeus formed black lightning in his hands and arced bolts at her. She deflected a few before forming a bubble around herself to absorb the rest. "Your pathetic attempts to resist are amusing, but we both know how this is going to end. So why don't you just give up?"

"I will never give up," Michelle said confidently, releasing the bubble around her.

"You can't win against me," Rubeus replied as he ricocheted some of her attacks away with just the flick of his wrist.

"Then come finish me off," Michelle challenged.

Rubeus hesitated for a moment. "I'm not falling for that," Rubeus said, crossing his arms.

"Falling for what?" Michelle asked. "You said yourself, I can't win. And you're right. I don't stand a chance against you."

"What is she doing?" Alyssa whispered.

"I'm not sure," Trevin whispered back.

"You're better than me," Michelle stated. Rubeus disappeared just as she tried to form a bubble around him. "Dammit." He reappeared behind her and grabbed ahold of her hair, yanking her head back. She cried out as he pushed her onto her knees.

"Nice try," Rubeus whispered in her ear.

"How could you possibly tell?" Michelle asked as she grabbed the hand that was holding her, trying to relieve some of the pressure.

"I can sense the shift in your energy," Rubeus explained as he tightened his grip. She arched her back slightly from the pain. "I know when you're about to use it."

"This is your last chance," Michelle stated.

Rubeus laughed. "*My* last chance? You are truly something else," Rubeus responded. "It's a shame I have to kill you. You were a nice challenge. We could have been great together. Any last requests?"

"Yeah, let me go," Michelle said.

"Try for something more realistic, sweetheart."

"All right," Michelle said. "How about a kiss?"

"That's...an odd request," Rubeus said, his grip loosening a bit.

"Nevertheless, that's my request."

"Why? To what purpose?" Rubeus asked.

"What's wrong? Too realistic for you, or you just can't deliver?" Michelle taunted.

Rubeus yanked her up and turned her to face him, without letting go of her hair. He studied her face for a moment, trying to get a feel for her energy. Sensing nothing, he leaned in and kissed her. Michelle kept it going as she wrapped her arms around his neck and let her essence flow around them. Rubeus let go of her hair as he embraced her back, her scent filling his senses. He opened his eyes as he realized she had put a bubble around them. "Gotcha," She whispered as she pulled away, her hands still on him, she pushed into his mind.

"No!" Rubeus cried out as he fell to his knees, bringing Michelle with him. He grabbed her hands. "Get out!"

She kept her grip on him as she closed her eyes and pushed deeper into his mind. He closed his eyes as well, retracting himself to try and resist, but she was already in too deep. Michelle stimulated the visual cortex and amygdala, two storage areas of long-term memories in the brain for sight and emotion, to force him to remember. Images of memories flashed through his mind, in chronological order, but worked their way backwards, starting with the most recent memories, until it stopped at the moment where he and Michelle first met at the café. The wind blew, and he grabbed her hat. They both opened their eyes and looked at each other the same way they did back then. She removed her hands but kept the bubble around them. Everyone watched, frozen, waiting to see if what she did had worked.

"Do you remember me?" Michelle whispered.

He put his hand on the side of her face. She closed her eyes, waiting, unsure of what he was going to do. "How could I forget you?" he whispered back. She opened her eyes, tears in them as he embraced her. She let the field drop, and everyone cheered.

"Welcome back," Trevin said as he and the others came up to them as they stood.

Rubeus looked around. "This place is a mess. What happened?"

"You happened," Trevin commented. "You went rampaging through the city looking for Michelle."

"You inhaled what looked like pollen when we were trying to get away from Dracul," Michelle informed. "Whatever that stuff was turned you against everyone."

"Did I hurt anyone?" Rubeus asked.

"There were a few causalities, but nothing that can't be healed," Camilla said.

"What about you?" he asked, looking back at Michelle.

"Besides you trying to kill me, I'm fine."

"And Dracul?" Remus questioned. "Where is he?"

"Bane said he'd deal with him," Michelle responded. "I'm not sure what he did."

"Bane?" Arixanna asked. "He's dead."

"I was brought back," Bane stated as he appeared. "Now that Dracul is taken care of, we need to seal him away."

He started into City Hall but stopped when he saw Ryan. He glanced back at Rubeus and then back to Ryan. Ryan crossed his arms.

"Surprised to see me?" Ryan asked.

"I spent years searching for you," Bane said. "You did a fine job hiding him from me, Remus."

"I did what needed to be done."

"No hard feelings, I hope." Bane extended his hand. Ryan glanced down at it and then back up to him.

"You think because you've temporarily stopped Dracul, you'll be liberated from your previous actions, and we'll all forgive you?" Ryan asked.

Bane shrugged and went to the entrance. He looked back at him. "The only one who matters has."

"I never said I forgave you," Michelle responded.

"No, but you're the only one here with the capacity to," Bane said. "Rubeus, will you please come with me?" He went into City Hall.

Rubeus started to follow, but Michelle grabbed his wrist. He looked back at her.

"He turned you against us, and you're just gonna follow him?" Michelle asked.

"I'll be fine," Rubeus reassured her as he tried to pull out of her grasp. "If you don't hear from me in fifteen minutes, then come for me." She let him go, and he went inside.

"She has nothing to worry about," Bane said as Rubeus walked up to him. He was waiting by the elevator.

"After what you did, she has every right to be," Rubeus replied. "What do you want?"

"I'm going to show you a spell you need," Bane said. "It's hidden away in my…your office. You're going to need help with it."

The doors to the elevator opened, and he stepped inside. He held the door until Rubeus joined him. It was a silent ride up to the top floor.

***

"You're just going to let Rubeus go in alone with him?" Alyssa asked.

"I'm going to trust him and give him the fifteen minutes," Michelle replied.

Alyssa shook her head and started to walk away. Suddenly Michelle grabbed ahold of her abdomen and fell to her knees. Alyssa turned back around.

"Are you okay?" she asked. Michelle couldn't say anything. Alyssa looked down at the ground. There were drops of water beneath Michelle. "Oh, God. Ryan!" Ryan looked over from talking with the other elders and saw Michelle on the ground. He ran over to them. "I think her water just broke." Michelle cried out as he scooped her up and pulled the necklace off her. The others gasped at the sight of her pregnant.

"I'm taking her to the hospital," Ryan said. He disappeared with her.

CHAPTER 37

Bane stepped up to the desk and pressed the button under it. The far wall opened. Rubeus followed him into the room as he started looking through the books.

"The book I need is missing," Bane said.

"Sven and Camilla pulled some things out awhile back," Rubeus informed. "They should be in one of the side rooms. I just haven't put them back yet."

Bane looked back at him. "You knew about this room?"

"Oh yeah," Rubeus replied. "I was all over this place when I was trying to see if you had any information on the location of McCain or how to contact him." They walked out of the room. "I also know about that portal to the castle." Rubeus walked off to the room that branched off to the left.

"I sealed that off centuries ago," Bane said.

"Well, I found it," Rubeus stated. "Is that how you snuck off to see Nerissa?"

"We had relations, if that's what you're getting at," Bane replied, ignoring his attempt to anger him. "I ended it when I found out what her true plans were. Where are these books?"

"On the table," Rubeus nodded. Bane moved past him and started looking at the book covers. He pulled one away from the rest and opened it. "So, how did you get Dracul to back off?"

Bane stopped at a page and pushed the book towards Rubeus. "Your blood is killing him, and Nerissa has an elixir for it, but it's not a permanent fix," Bane informed him. "I told him that if he left you two alone, I would be sure to keep him in a supply of it."

"How? Nerissa isn't just going to give it up," Rubeus replied as he read through the ingredients.

"We're going to break into her supply and get the ingredients we need to make it," Bane stated.

"She'll be able to sense our presence there," Rubeus responded. "There's no way."

"And that's where your little friend comes in," Bane replied. "Alyssa will distract her long enough for us to get in and get out."

"Why should I trust you?" Rubeus asked, looking at his watch.

"Because I want Dracul gone just as much as you do," Bane said.

Alyssa and Trevin came into the room. Rubeus followed Bane's gaze and turned around.

"Where's Michelle?" Rubeus asked.

"She and Ryan went to go check something out," Alyssa said. "She'll be back…in a day or so."

"What are they looking into that takes more than a day?" Rubeus asked.

"You know, they didn't really get into it," Alyssa answered. "Did you find what you need?"

"Yeah, but—" Rubeus started.

"Great, let's go." Alyssa turned and left.

Rubeus looked to Trevin, but he only shrugged his

shoulders. The three walked out into the main office to find Alyssa was already gone.

"So, what's the plan?" Trevin asked.

"Well, first, we need to make a list of what we need to steal from Nerissa's pantry," Rubeus said.

"I'm sorry, what?" Trevin questioned.

"Only she has what we need," Bane responded.

"Alyssa needs to distract her so we can get it," Rubeus said.

"Oh, is that it?" Trevin asked, a little sarcastically.

"I know it's crazy, but it's all we got," Rubeus said.

CHAPTER 38

Alyssa knocked on the door to Michelle's room in the hospital. She didn't get a response but came in anyway. Michelle was asleep. Alyssa dropped a bag by the bed and sat in the chair next to it, placing her hand on hers. Michelle woke from the contact.

"Hey," Alyssa said. "Are you okay?"

"Yeah." Michelle stretched. "I should be released today."

"And the baby?" Alyssa asked.

"A month early, but he's fine," Michelle answered. "Remus is going to keep him until I tell Rubeus."

"You should have—" Alyssa started.

Michelle put her hand up, stopping her. "I don't need to be lectured on what I should have done. I'll tell him."

"Kind of need to now," Alyssa snapped without meaning to. Michelle shook her head and sighed. "I'm sorry. I told Rubeus you and Ryan went to look into something, and it may take a few days. I know he doesn't believe me, but I didn't know what else to tell him."

"I'll come up with something," Michelle said. "Is there any news on how to get rid of Dracul?"

"There are some ingredients we need that only Nerissa

has," Alyssa said. "They want me to distract her so they can get them."

"What are they waiting on?" Michelle asked.

"We're trying to let things die down a little before going for it," Alyssa replied. "And I'm trying to come up with a reason to see her."

"That's simple," Michelle said, sitting up. "Tell her you've had a change of heart."

"I don't know if I could pull that off," Alyssa admitted.

"Should be easy," Michelle commented. "You've been lying to me since I've known you."

"I've apologized for that," Alyssa said, getting upset. "But that was different—I wasn't conspiring against you."

"You withheld things because Nerissa told you to," Michelle stated. "So technically, you were."

"I didn't know what her plans were," Alyssa rebutted. "How is this even relevant right now?"

"Because you could still be lying."

"I don't want anything to happen to anyone here or this realm," Alyssa said. "Believe it or not, I have a lot to lose too."

"I know you do," Michelle responded. No one spoke for a few minutes. "So, what kind of force field needs ingredients?"

"I've been trying to wrap my mind around that too," Alyssa said. They were both unaware that they were going for the ingredients to keep Dracul alive. "I don't trust Bane. I think he's going for something else."

A nurse came in with Michelle's release papers. She signed them, and Alyssa handed her a change of clothes she had brought from the manor. They both left the hospital room, and Michelle started heading towards the main entrance to leave.

"What about the baby?"

"Remus already took him," Michelle said. "He was released yesterday, but they wanted to keep me another day."

"What are you gonna tell Rubeus?" Alyssa asked.

"I'm not sure yet," Michelle confessed. "It's my problem, not yours."

As soon as they stepped outside, Michelle disappeared.

Michelle reappeared outside the manor. She paused, looking up at it, before going inside. She wasn't looking forward to the conversation she was about to have with Rubeus. He was going to be livid.

As soon as she stepped inside, she immediately heard Rubeus and Trevin talking in the study upstairs. She sighed and slowly made her way up the stairs and turned right, down the little balcony that overlooked the main foyer. Michelle stood outside a moment before entering, trying to get her thoughts together. Just as she was about to walk in, they both came out.

"Hey," Rubeus said. "When did you get back?"

"Just now," Michelle answered. "Can we talk?"

Rubeus looked at his watch. "Right now?" he asked. "I need to meet Bane." Michelle's expression and mood immediately changed. "As soon as we get back, I promise." He gave her a quick kiss and vanished down the steps and out the door with Trevin.

Michelle stared vacantly at the floor, at a loss for words. She was expecting him to lay into her with questions of where she had gone and why. She couldn't help but wonder if he knew as she went into the study and sat down on one of the couches. Michelle glanced over at an open book on the coffee table in front of her and saw some highlighting in it.

She leaned closer to it to see what it was. There was a list of ingredients in the middle of the page. Michelle grabbed the book and read through it.

"He's going to get them killed," Michelle said to herself. She put the book down and disappeared.

CHAPTER 39

"Alyssa, I'm so glad you're here," Nerissa said with a smile as she saw Alyssa enter the castle. "I have something I need to discuss with you."

"Great, I need to speak with you as well," Alyssa responded, her nerves starting to get to her.

"Follow me." Nerissa started down a hallway that branched off to the left. It happened to go by her pantry of spell ingredients.

"How about we just talk right here?" Alyssa asked as she caught up to her and grabbed ahold of her elbow. Nerissa turned and looked at her.

"I suppose we could," Nerissa said. She made her way to the great room where everyone had gathered before when the realms were falling apart. Nerissa took a seat while Alyssa continued to stand. "You look nervous."

"I'm just not sure how to start," Alyssa admitted.

"Start by having a seat and a drink," Nerissa suggested. She got up and grabbed a bottle of wine. She poured them both a glass and sat back down. Alyssa sat across from her and took a sip.

"Okay, so…," Alyssa started. "I'm sorry, this is difficult for me."

Nerissa sat her glass down and leaned over towards her. She reached out and touched her knee. "It's okay. You can tell me," Nerissa said, showing genuine concern.

"I just wanted to say that I'm sorry for always going against you," Alyssa said. "And that you have my full support from here on out."

"You have no idea how pleased I am to hear that." Nerissa smiled. "It fits perfectly with what I need to talk to you about."

"Oh?" Alyssa asked, unsure how to feel about it.

"I need you to find Celeste and give her something for me," Nerissa said.

"Celeste?" Alyssa asked, a little confused.

"Yes," Nerissa answered. "If you'll excuse me, I need to go grab something from my pantry." She started to get up.

"Hold on a minute," Alyssa said in a panic. Nerissa looked at her. "Let me get it for you."

"You don't know what it is, dear," Nerissa replied. She got up and left.

Alyssa immediately got out her phone.

***

"Did you get what you needed?" Rubeus asked as he looked out into the hallway. "She's on the way."

"Yes," Bane responded. "Let's go."

They rounded the corner and headed towards the stairs to go back through the portal just as Nerissa came from the other side. She went into her pantry and grabbed a crystal vial. On her way out, she glimpsed something in the corner — a long-stemmed blue rose. She picked it up as a small smile formed.

"You're alive," Nerissa whispered as she smelled it.

Alyssa nervously waited for a reply to her text when

Nerissa walked back in. She looked up and put her phone away. They had obviously made it out without her seeing them. Nerissa approached and handed her the crystal vial.

"I need you to give this to Celeste when you find her," Nerissa said. "All she has to do is drink it, and I'll take care of the rest when the time is right."

"What does it do?" Alyssa asked as she took the vial and looked at it.

"That's nothing you need to concern yourself with."

"How am I supposed to find her?" Alyssa questioned. "She doesn't have an energy signature for me to focus on."

"Of course she does," Nerissa replied. "Stripping someone's power doesn't take their energy signature away."

"I thought it made you human," Alyssa said.

"Not genetically — she's still a demon," Nerissa explained. "If Aiden were to use his second sight on her, her aura would still be blue, just not as bright." Nerissa turned and grabbed her glass of wine. "I wouldn't ask this of you if I didn't trust you. What you said earlier showed me I can." She took a sip and looked back at her. "It's imperative that you find her immediately. Don't leave until you see her drink it, then report back to me that she has."

"I'll get right on it then."

***

Michelle was leaning against the table in the hidden room in Rubeus's office with her arms crossed when he and Bane stepped through the portal. Bane nodded at her as he made his way out of the room and towards the side room to the left. Rubeus started to follow, but Michelle grabbed his arm.

"You do realize that you don't need ingredients to make a force field, right?" Michelle asked.

"Yeah," Rubeus answered.

"Then what did you need?" Michelle inquired.

"We need to make the elixir that Nerissa was giving Dracul to keep my blood from killing him," Rubeus said. "It's the deal Bane made with him to keep him off us."

"All we need to do to keep him off us is to get that field up," Michelle argued. "That needs to happen as soon as possible."

"This coming from the one who disappeared for a few days," Rubeus commented. Michelle started to say something, but he cut her off. "This is going to show us exactly where we need to create the field." He held out a little crystal and left the room. Before joining Bane, he turned around. "You know, you could…."

He stopped and looked around. Michelle was gone. An annoyed expression formed on his face as he shook his head and entered the side room.

CHAPTER 40

Alyssa appeared outside a cave in the human realm, at the base of the mountains of the Blue Forest. She pulled out the crystal vial, still wondering what it was and what it did. She had pulled the stopper off it shortly after Nerissa had given it to her and smelled it, but it had no odor. It was a pearl color and had a consistency like molten silver. Alyssa had tried to look up what it could be based off that but couldn't find anything. Whatever it was, Nerissa didn't want anyone knowing. She slipped it back into her pocket and headed into the cave.

Celeste looked up when she heard someone coming. She hid in the shadows as she saw Alyssa come in.

"Celeste?" Alyssa called out.

"How did you find me?" Celeste asked, stepping out of the shadows.

"I'm the Apostle. I can find anyone," Alyssa stated.

"You replaced McCain?" Celeste asked.

Alyssa nodded. "He was my father."

"What? He never mentioned any kids to me," Celeste said, surprised.

"I didn't know either, and I'm pretty sure neither did he," Alyssa said. "I have something for you." She pulled the vial out. "It's from Nerissa."

Celeste approached her and took the offered vial. "Could it be?" Celeste asked herself as she pulled the stopper off. She looked inside and sniffed it. Her eyes lit up as she drank it. "I don't feel any different."

"Well, she said all you had to do was drink it, and she would take care of the rest when the time was right."

"Of course, she would keep some kind of control with it," Celeste replied. "I guess let her know I'm ready when she is."

"Will do," Alyssa said, taking the empty vial before disappearing.

***

"She drank it," Alyssa stated as she handed Nerissa the empty vial. "She said she's ready when you are."

"Perfect." Nerissa smiled.

"What was that stuff?" Alyssa asked again.

"I told you, you don't need to worry about that."

"Does it give her her power back?" Alyssa asked.

"She thinks it will, but it doesn't," Nerissa said. "She'll be making a great sacrifice for the greater good. Thank you."

Nerissa walked out of the room. Alyssa stood frozen for just a second before disappearing. She couldn't help but think she'd just helped Nerissa do something terrible.

CHAPTER 41

It took about a month for the elixir to ferment. Bane was doing the finishing touches with it while Rubeus gathered the elders. Alyssa couldn't be found; she had disappeared shortly after completing Nerissa's task. She didn't even tell Trevin where she went. Michelle still hadn't told Rubeus about their child and disappeared several times a day without an explanation of where she was going. She thought he didn't notice since he was busy with other things, but he did—he just chose not to say anything. Everyone was stressed, and it was an argument he didn't have the energy for.

Everyone gathered at the edge of the banana trees on the other side of the realm. Rubeus had gone out earlier with the crystal he had and marked the location where the field had to be created. They were just waiting for Bane to return from giving Dracul several months' worth of elixir. Dracul didn't know they were putting the field back up, sealing his fate once he ran out of the elixir.

Alyssa appeared while they were waiting.

"Where have you been?" Trevin asked.

"I'm sorry," Alyssa answered. "I should've let you know, but I had something I needed to deal with on my own. I didn't want to burden you with it."

"Whatever you were dealing with, it wouldn't have been a burden," Trevin responded.

"What did you do?" Michelle asked.

Alyssa looked over at her. "I had to do a task for Nerissa," Alyssa admitted. "If I refused, it would have proved that she couldn't trust me."

"Who cares if she trusts you?" Rubeus commented.

"Well, my distraction for you was telling her that I had a change in heart and supported her," Alyssa retorted. "She would have caught you if I didn't come up with something."

"What was your task?" Michelle inquired.

"I had to find Celeste and give her some kind of potion," Alyssa answered. "I don't know what it was or what it does. Nerissa wouldn't tell me, and I couldn't find it anywhere."

"Of course she wouldn't tell you," Rubeus said as Bane finally came back. "You probably just gave Celeste her power back."

"Nerissa said it didn't," Alyssa replied. "Celeste was meant to think that, but it's some kind of sacrifice."

"Right," Rubeus said, not believing any of it. "We'll deal with this later." He turned to Bane.

"Are we ready?" Bane asked.

"Let's do this," Michelle said.

Rubeus put the crystal on the marked spot as everyone formed a half circle around it. They closed their eyes as their bodies glowed with energy. Everyone's power combined, creating a shield at the entrance of the cave. The ground started to rumble as another shield started to shoot up along the border between the beach and the brush line in both directions. The two ends met at the crystal and sealed together with a brilliant flash of light, blasting everyone back. Rubeus sat up and looked around as everyone else started to come to.

"Where's Michelle?" Rubeus asked once everyone was up. Everyone started looking around.

"I don't know," Camilla said. "She was standing right—"

"No," Rubeus whispered when he saw where she was pointing. It was on the other side of the shield. "That can't be possible."

"If she was standing on the other side when the shield went up, it is," Bane replied.

Rubeus glared over at him. "This is *your* doing."

"I had nothing to do with it," Bane snapped. "I thought I had proved my intentions."

"Old habits die hard, I guess. Take him to the Hollows," Rubeus ordered. Camilla and Sven grabbed ahold of him.

"On what grounds?" Bane demanded.

"You used truth serum to turn me against everyone," Rubeus said.

"I wasn't the one who used it," Bane countered.

"And I'm supposed to believe that?" Rubeus asked. "Take him away."

Bane pulled out of their grasp and disappeared.

"Should we track him?" Camilla asked.

"No," Rubeus said. "It'll only be a matter of time before he strikes again."

Everyone disappeared except for Trevin and Alyssa.

Rubeus looked over at her. "How can I get through?" He stepped up to the shield and put his hand on it.

"You can't," Alyssa said. "It's impenetrable."

He closed his eyes. "There has to be a way."

"I'm sorry, but if that's where she really is, then she's stuck over there," Alyssa replied. "The shield may weaken eventually, but that could take centuries."

Rubeus pounded his fists against the shield, energy rippling out across it.

"If the cave is sealed, then what purpose does this shield have?" Trevin asked.

"An extra protective measure," Rubeus informed. He formed energy and threw it at the shield. It absorbed into it and spit it back out at him. The energy slammed into him, tossing him back. He landed hard on his back, the wind knocked out of him.

"Another protective measure," Alyssa commented. "We should go."

"You can go if you want," Rubeus said. "I'm not leaving."

"You're wasting your time," Alyssa said. "There's just no way. She's lost to us."

Rubeus was silent for a moment. "I'll catch up to you then."

Trevin and Alyssa disappeared.

"There's gotta be a weak point somewhere," Rubeus said out loud to himself as he looked up at the shield.

CHAPTER 42

Michelle came to and pushed up on her hands. She looked around at her surroundings and then saw the shield.

"No," she whispered as she stood up and ran to it. She pushed on it and then started slamming her fists into it. Michelle formed energy in her hands and emitted a stream of lightning at it. The entire shield rippled before throwing it back out at her. She twisted out of the way just in time. "There's gotta be a way." Michelle spent a few more hours trying to find a way through the shield before finally giving up. She went back to the cabin to rest before trying again the next day.

Michelle lost track of how long she had been trapped on the other side, but she didn't give up on trying to find a weak point in the shield. She was on her way to another section of the shield when she saw movement. She looked around and saw the cave. Michelle hadn't realized she was that close to it. Dracul had somehow broken out of the force field at the entrance and was watching her from the top of the cave. He almost reminded her of a gargoyle the way he was perched.

"Your attempts won't work," Dracul stated. "I've tried many times." He jumped down and started to approach her. Michele formed energy in her palms. "Don't worry, I won't hurt you."

"I beg to differ," Michelle said. "I'm surprised you're still alive."

"Bane kept up his end, except for the sealing me away part. He only gave me enough to last a few months. I should've known," Dracul said with melancholy, accepting his fate. Neither of them spoke for a few minutes. "You know, your species is a lot more powerful than you think. Even more than Nerissa in some respects."

"I find that hard to believe," Michelle replied.

"If you knew the truth about your species, you'd have a better understanding."

"And how exactly would you know?" Michelle questioned. "You weren't around at the beginning. Your only purpose is to destroy us."

"That's where you're wrong," Dracul stated. "Do you know the real reason behind my kind's creation? The real reason why Nerissa wants all purebloods destroyed?"

"If she wanted us destroyed, then why did she help save Rubeus when he was born?" Michelle asked.

"You would have to speak with Nerissa to find out her reasoning with that," Dracul said. "I was long gone by then."

"Okay, so let's say you're telling the truth," Michelle said, crossing her arms. "What's the real reason?"

"She found out that purebloods could absorb power," Dracul explained. "That's how your kind became so powerful. You have the ability to wipe out her entire race."

Michelle turned away. "She did mention that only Rubeus and I could share power," Michelle remembered. She looked back at him. "Is that part of it?"

"Yes," Dracul answered. "And now that you've somehow served your purpose, she wants to be rid of you, along with everyone else."

"Why was Bane helping her then?" Michelle asked mainly herself. "Why does he want his own species destroyed?"

"I don't want our species destroyed," Bane said. "I've always been trying to stop Nerissa."

Michelle and Dracul looked over and saw Bane and Alyssa.

"How did you get here?" Michelle asked.

"I apparently have the power to create and destroy that shield," Alyssa responded. Michelle looked to Bane. "If you're trying to stop her, why did you send Rubeus after me?" Michelle inquired.

"I wasn't the one who used the truth serum," Bane said. "That was Nerissa. Putting it in a powder form was genius on her part."

"I don't understand why she wants us gone if she wanted us to survive," Michelle said.

"It was all part of her plan," Bane replied. "She saw a prophecy about the realms collapsing and that only two purebloods could save it. She saw it as an opportunity to release the demon hunters once again and finish us off. Nerissa shared this with me and wanted me to join her, but I refused."

"That's the real reason you went after demons who could have purebloods?" Michelle asked. "To save the rest of the species."

"Yes," Bane admitted. "But unfortunately, I ended up aiding her anyway when I set McCain up. I didn't know his hatred would grow to the point where Rubeus would end up killing him, which is what she ultimately wanted. She knew his death would cause the collapse."

"We have to get to the space between the realms before it's too late," Alyssa reminded them.

"Why? What's happening?" Michelle asked.

"Rubeus went there to confront her," Alyssa answered.

"You should be worried for Nerissa then," Michelle commented.

"She has the power to kill him," Alyssa stated.

"She can't," Michelle said, not believing it. "It goes against the agreement."

"Not if he attacks first," Alyssa said. "Self-defense."

"Will you take me there?" Michelle asked.

"Of course," Alyssa said. She took Michelle's hand.

"I need to make one stop first," Michelle requested. "How long have I been gone?"

"It's been a week," Alyssa responded. "Where do you need to go?"

"The mansion," Michelle said. "I need to check on my son."

They disappeared.

CHAPTER 43

Rubeus had gone through the portal in his office to get to the space between the realms. He found Nerissa in an open room in the castle.

"What do you want?" Nerissa asked without turning around.

Bane arrived shortly after Michelle and Alyssa disappeared from behind the force field. He saw Rubeus and hid in one of the side rooms.

"I want you to lower the field so I can bring Michelle back," Rubeus ordered, not knowing Alyssa had the ability to do it.

"You've already stolen from me, so why should I help you?" Nerissa asked. "I don't want her back anyway."

"Because your other option involves your death," Rubeus threatened.

"How dare you come into *my* home and threaten me," Nerissa said as she whipped around. "You forget...," Nerissa started. "I gave you that enzyme, and I can take it back."

Rubeus cried out, falling to the floor as Nerissa shot her arm out towards him, pulling the enzyme from his body with energy. A bubble formed around Nerissa, stopping the energy. She quickly turned and gasped when she saw Michelle approaching her. Rubeus looked over and was shocked to see her.

"You look surprised to see me," Michelle responded. "Planning on me being stuck on the other side for a while?" She stopped in front of her.

"Perhaps we can talk about this," Nerissa said.

"No, we're past that," Michelle replied. She reached through the bubble and grabbed ahold of the side of Nerissa's face. The bubble disappeared.

"You should have kept me in that," Nerissa said with a smile. Her smile quickly faded when she realized she couldn't teleport.

"What's wrong, Nerissa?" Michelle asked.

"How are you doing that?" Nerissa questioned as she tried to teleport again.

"Doing what? Preventing you from getting away?" Michelle leaned in towards her. "Just a little mind trick I learned." Nerissa's eyes widened. "I've learned something else too." Nerissa formed energy in her free hand. Michelle glanced down at it and smiled. "You think you're faster than my thoughts?" Nerissa saw the newfound knowledge in her eyes. The energy in her hand disappeared as she tried to pull Michelle's hand off her.

"No, please," Nerissa begged, tears in her eyes. Her natural glow faded as Michelle started to drain her energy. Nerissa fell to the ground as she let her go. Michelle fell to her knees as she tried to add the energy to herself.

"It's too much for you," Alyssa said. "Give it to me."

Michelle shook her head. She drew the energy into an orb in her palms.

"No one needs this kind of power," Michelle stated. "Put it in a safe place." She handed it to Alyssa.

"How did you do that?" Rubeus asked as he sat up, still in pain.

"I was told," Michelle said. "I knew there was a reason she kept her distance from us. Why you and I and are the only ones who can pull each other's energy. The reason purebloods became so powerful is because we could take their power. Which is the real reason behind the creation of the realms and the manipulation of our DNA."

Nerissa glared up at her. "It didn't get rid of you."

"That's why you created the demon hunters," Michelle responded. "But you didn't know they would attack your people too. It forced you to join with us to beat them back and banish them."

"Which is why the Apostle was really created," Alyssa added. "The peacekeeping between the realms was just a front. The Apostle is really the guardian of that rift, to keep the demon hunters from emerging."

"Looks like you have it all figured out," Nerissa said.

"If you wanted to be rid of us so bad, then why let Michelle and I live?" Rubeus asked.

"Because I knew Bane's desperate need to stop me would eventually lead to the corruption of McCain," Nerissa explained. "You and Michelle were only born as purebloods because I wanted it. With McCain's death, the realms would fall apart, and only purebloods would be able to save it. I knew it would release Dracul, so I would be rid of you along with the other demons as well. With you all gone, I would finally be able to let my people leave this place and live normal lives in the human realm like they were originally meant to"

"You can still do that," Alyssa said. "We can all live together in peace."

"Never." Nerissa put one of her hands in her pocket.

"You may have taken my energy, but I can still at least get rid of one of you." She flung some of the enzyme mixed with blood she still had in her hand from Rubeus at Michelle while crushing a crystal she had in her pocket with her other hand. Her body flashed quick enough that no one noticed since their focus was on Michelle. The blood hit Michelle in the face and eyes.

"*Noooo!*" Rubeus cried out as Michelle fell. He immersed Nerissa in demon fire as he got up and went to Michelle.

Nerissa screamed as the fire engulfed her. "You tricked me!" she yelled.

Michelle started to shake as her body temperature drastically dropped, then began to vomit violently before passing out. Rubeus grabbed Michelle.

"Get me out of here!" Rubeus yelled. Alyssa grabbed his arm and disappeared with them.

CHAPTER 44

"The fact that she isn't dead is astounding." Ryan put a blood sample under the microscope. Michelle was wrapped up in blankets in their bed. Her body was freezing, and her skin had a bluish tint to it. Rubeus was standing away from them with his arms crossed, a worried expression on his face. "Your enzyme is clearly in her blood, but it looks like she's built-up resistance to it."

"Well, what does that mean?" Rubeus inquired.

"Your blood can't harm her." Ryan turned to him. "She just received too much at once and has to overcome it."

"How did she build a resistance to it?" Rubeus asked.

"From being with you," Ryan stated. "That enzyme is in all your bodily fluids. It's just more concentrated and toxic in your blood. The pregnancy helped boost her immunity to it greatly."

"Pregnancy?" Rubeus asked. "You mean the one she lost?"

"No, I mean your son," Ryan answered. "She never told you?"

"No, I had no idea," Rubeus said.

Ryan started packing his things up. "Well, I'm sorry you found out from me. She said she was going to tell you shortly after he was born."

"How could I not know?" Rubeus wondered. "There were no symptoms. She never showed."

Ryan tossed a charm at him. "She's apparently very talented. That charm disguised her appearance and symptoms."

"Well, where is he?" Rubeus asked.

"The human realm in the mansion, with Remus," Ryan said.

"What about Michelle?" Rubeus inquired.

"She's going to be fine," he said as he put his hand on his shoulder on his way out. "Give her a couple of days, and she'll be as good as new."

***

Rubeus went to the mansion in the human realm. He debated knocking on the door or just barging in. Just as he was about to open the door, Remus opened it for him.

"I was wondering when you were going to show up."

"I would've come sooner if I had known," Rubeus replied.

"Michelle never told you?" Remus questioned as he held the door open for him. Rubeus stepped inside.

"Obviously not." Remus shook his head as he shut the door. He followed him to the left and down a hallway to the room Remus had the baby in. "I can't believe she felt she needed to hide this from me."

"You must have really done something to make her afraid to tell you," Remus said. "Even after that misunderstanding you had."

"It was never my intention," Rubeus replied, looking into the crib. The baby was sleeping.

"His name is Blake," Remus said.

"When did she have him?" Rubeus asked.

"A little over a month ago, I guess," Remus answered. "It was shortly after her battle with you."

Rubeus thought back and remembered Alyssa saying Michelle left to take care of something but never said what. She had been gone for a few days and continued to randomly disappear several times during the day, thinking he wouldn't notice.

"I should have figured it out." Rubeus shook his head. "She kept disappearing, and I never asked where she kept going. I didn't want to start another fight."

"Well, don't be too upset with her," Remus responded.

"I'm not," Rubeus stated. "This is my own doing."

Remus gave him a shocked look. "You've really amazed me lately," Remus admitted. "I can't believe how you've handled these past events. Granted, your temper still gets away from you, but you've really matured."

"Being responsible for so many lives will do it to you," Rubeus replied. "I've never had so many look to me for answers and to keep them safe."

"Being an elder is a big responsibility on its own, but head elder, that's an entirely different game," Remus said. "I certainly wouldn't be able to do it."

"She's the true head elder. I should be second to her," Rubeus said as he lightly brushed the side of Blake's face. He opened his eyes. "She has way more power than I do."

"Well, she's just now realizing her true potential," Remus stated. "Who knows, maybe she'll challenge you once she figures that out."

"And she'd win," Rubeus replied, smiling when Blake grabbed his finger. "Every time."

CHAPTER 45

"Nerissa is dead," a woman announced, entering a hideaway deep underground. Sierra, Rachel, and Melissa turned to see who the intruder was.

"Who are *you*?" Rachel questioned, preparing to defend them.

"And how did you find us?" Sierra asked.

The woman stepped into the light. The girls gasped.

"Celeste," Melissa stated. "We thought you were dead."

"No, Rubeus' attack was poorly aimed," Celeste informed. "I didn't take a direct hit."

"How did you find out about Nerissa?" Rachel questioned.

"Someone as powerful as her dies. The realms feel it," Celeste replied.

"Why are you here then?" Sierra inquired.

"Her power is up for grabs at the castle," Celeste explained. "I want it. And you're going to help me get it."

"Why would we help you?" Melissa crossed her arms.

"Because I can help you get revenge on Michelle and Rubeus with it."

"We could just take it for ourselves," Sierra responded.

"You don't have the connections I have to get close enough," Celeste countered.

"They'll be expecting something this soon," Rachel said.

"How patient are you?" Celeste asked with a smile.

Heather is a Virginia resident who started writing when she was 15. She grew up in Maryland with an older sister and traveled over the U.S. while serving in the Army. Her favorite past times include writing, traveling, biking/hiking and just being near the water. She has no children but is the proud mother of a rambunctious dog and two ornery cats. She has a Culinary Arts and Radiologic Sciences degree and currently works as an MRI Technologist at Chippenham Medical Center.

www.ingramcontent.com/pod-product-compliance
Lightning Source LLC
Chambersburg PA
CBHW030332180626
46810CB00003B/1325